T0115086

THE LIFE
AND
ADVENTURES OF
JODIE

JIMMY GREY EAGLE

IUNIVERSE, INC.
BLOOMINGTON

The Life and Adventures of Jodie

This is a work of fiction. All of the characters, names, incidents, organizations, and dialogue in this novel are either the products of the author's imagination or are used fictitiously.

iUniverse books may be ordered through booksellers or by contacting:

iUniverse
1663 Liberty Drive
Bloomington, IN 47403
www.iuniverse.com
1-800-Authors (1-800-288-4677)

Because of the dynamic nature of the Internet, any web addresses or links contained in this book may have changed since publication and may no longer be valid. The views expressed in this work are solely those of the author and do not necessarily reflect the views of the publisher, and the publisher hereby disclaims any responsibility for them.

Any people depicted in stock imagery provided by Thinkstock are models, and such images are being used for illustrative purposes only.

Certain stock imagery © Thinkstock.

ISBN: 978-1-4502-9982-4 (sc)
ISBN: 978-1-4502-9984-8 (dj)
ISBN: 978-1-4502-9983-1 (ebk)

Printed in the United States of America

iUniverse rev. date: 2/15/2011

CONTENTS

A BEGINNING

Chapter One

The old flat bottom riverboat rocked a little as the wind shifted out of the East. It had been some kind of bad storm just about all night, but for the last couple of hours things had been still as the dead.

The young boy of maybe sixteen years, eyes popped open. His eyes felt like they were full of sand. He had just fought hard for several hours just to stay afloat. He was worn slap dab out and was sore all over from all the strain on his body. His head felt like someone was using it for a drum. Everything in the cabin was soaking wet. As he lay there trying to come fully awake, he listened; finally he heard the bowline squeak as it tightened up against the boat. He slowly closed his eyes and passed out once again.

It was at night when his eyes opened again. He could hear voices outside coming from somewhere not too far away.

He quickly stood and eased outside trying to see who the voices belonged to in the darkness. Finally, he recognized the voice of Pennyfellow, the sheriff of Holmes County. He was telling the other fellow whose name was Berk Longs what he thought. Jodie stood silently in the pitch-black darkness and listened.

"Look here Berk, I know how bad you won't to hang that sawed off little bastard for killing your top hand but we already lost two good men in that damn storm, Bill Cooley and James Snips, and sides my boat is all busted up and is full of water. And there ain't no way in hell that runaway could have survived that kind of storm. So I'm a thinking we should head on home and..."

Longs broke in. "Hell I reckon your right. We still got a couple of long poles ain't we?

"You damn right we have and your riverboat." said Sheriff Pennyfellow.

"Then what in tar nation are we waiting fer?" Let's head back; we should make it back to Bonifay by day after tomorrow. We can get drunk and grab a couple of them Gouge gals and have us a party."

" Berk, you old dog you know we done went and run them gals out of town for lose living."

"Sheriff some people will do about anything to get re-elected..."snickered Long.

You could tell by the way they sounded they had already been a pulling the cork. Jodie could almost see them getting into Berk's short little riverboat. Then he heard a huge splash.

"Is the water cold sheriff?" Berk asked laughing.

"Hell yea, but it ain't very deep."

" Well you best be getting back in the boat before one of those blue crabs makes a girl out of you."

He heard the sheriff scramble back in the boat, and the two of them take off for Holmes County.

A nice warm breeze was blowing out of the East, as Jodie stretched out on the deck and placed his hands under his head. He tried to fall back to sleep, but his head was packed tighter than a drum. It was full of the things that had happened the last three days, well actually the last four days.

He was thinking about how it all began, he was shooting dice between Bull Lang's Hardware and Farley's Bar. I had done won two dollars and thirty-seven cents. You might say I was right lucky at shooting dice. Then that jackass Robert Willard tossed a waded up (what appeared to be a dollar bill) down and said...

"Cover that if you can street rat."

I looked up at him and said. "Unwad it."

Oh, I almost forgot, Robert Willard was Mr. Berk Long's top hand. Now old Robert was famous for wadding a piece of colored paper, throwing it down, and calling it a dollar and if you touched it, he would say you switched it and took his money. So I told him again.

"You unwad your money or there ain't no bet!"

He went and got mad as a wet setting hen. I knew he was bad about kicking people in the head when he could. So I went and sprang to my feet like a long tail tomcat falling off the porch. He jumped back and cried out, "You call me a cheat?"

I told him, "damn right I am!"

Well he was all over me like tire at a KKK meeting. Somehow, he got my hands behind me and one of his buddy's, James Snips done went and whipped out a long bladed butcher knife and lunged at me. But I did a Jodie run around and James stuck that butcher knife slap dab up to the hilt in Robert's chest. Everybody ran but me.

I was busily gathering up my money. I could hear old Snips running down Main Street crying out at the top of his lungs, "Jodie done went and killed Robert Willard, stabbed him plumb through with a butcher knife."

So I grabbed my money and headed for the Chackahatchey River, and an old riverboat that used to belong to an old friend of mine who had fell over board and drowned five days ago. It took no time at all and I was on board the riverboat and headed for the Gulf of Mexico.

I could hear some of the town folk a hollering, "He's headed down the river in Old Man Bubling's boat, get the Sheriff.

I felt good hearing that. I would be way down river, before the sheriff could even get started.

It was late the third day, I was just fixing to enter the Gulf when I heard a commotion on the right bank. It was the Sheriff and Mr. Longs, Cooley, and Snips. Snips was running up and down the bank screaming "There goes the bastard, shoot him, shoot him."

I sure was glad none of them could shoot worth a darn. I think everyone of them took at least one shot at me. I had old man Bubling's twelve gauge leaned up against the cabin door, but I couldn't find no powder and shot. But it looked good leaning there. Once I reached open waters, the wind was blowing out of the North pretty strong, so about all I had to do was skull it in the direction I wanted to go. And that was away from there.

It was almost breath taking; the speed the wind was carrying the small flat bottom boat. I looked back and only saw the Sheriff and his posse one time.

The rest you already know.

I was about two hours out and all hell broke loose. The wind was blowing so hard, it was slamming waves across the boat, almost washing me over board several times, as it shoved my boat towards the saw grass flats along the western shoreline of Florida. The next thing I knew I was doing everything I could do just to stay alive. Then I saw a large limb, through the storm and I grabbed it and tied the bowline to it. And prayed like heck that it would hold until this storm from the pits of hell blew over.

As dawn broke bright and clear, I am lying here on the deck of a flat boat in the middle of November, freezing and wet through to the bone. Wishing to God that I was somewhere's warm and dry.

AFTER THE STORM

Chapter Two

By the time, the sun got high enough to see, the wind had switched around out of the North East. Once Jodie had put most of the wet bedding out on the deck to dry, he was starting to feel hungry. He searched the tiny cabin for something to eat, old man Bublings must have not believed in storing up much food cause all he found was some beat up pots and pans, one of them being a frying pan, a large jar of corn meal and one of flour. And a two pound can of coffee, and another two pound can of lard. He also discovered a foot tub the old man used for a stove. He'd fill it about half full of wet sand and build a fire in it. The sand would not be a problem, seeing the water was not very deep at all here about. "But where the devil am I gonna get wood at?" He mumbled as he checked the water keg. It was full. His teeth were bumping together like a bunch of bullfrogs in a mason jar with shear cold as he looked down the edge of the saw grass, he could see the sheriff's abandoned flat boat. Just about the whole thing was out of the water, because the tide was going out.

Jodie went back inside the cabin, directly he appeared wearing a pair of wading boots. He slipped over the side and headed for the old boat. By the time he made it to the boat he was wore slap out, causing there was more mud than sand and he had to wade through it to get to the boat. And Gulf mud is the worst kind of mud to walk in it is more like a real thick gumbo than mud. He decided to just stretch out on the deck and just lay there for a long time.

Finally, he stood up and looked around; the bowline was stretching out behind the disabled boat. Jodie pulled the line in and coiled it up on the deck. Ropes are good trading stuff. The roof of the cabin was almost torn off all that kept it on was a few boards. So he finished tearing it off and placed it on the mud beside the boat, and placed the coil of rope on the old roof. The boat had lost one of its planks off the right side. The sheriff was right, she was a coming apart. There was a lot of good stuff in what was left of the cabin. Jodie worked hard stacking it on his makeshift sled. There were all kinds can goods. Mostly all beans. There was also a slab of pork and a half of smoked ham and a round of cheese, an unopened keg of crackers, man this was turning into a good snag

He all of a sudden felt the wind as it picked up, then the rain, ice-cold rain. He took one last look around.

There was a small wooden box with a cover on it, what the heck, he grabbed it and away he went. He wasted no time getting back on his riverboat, grabbed his bedding and tossed it in the cabin. Then he took everything he had salvaged inside and closed the door.

To his surprise the cabin wasn't cold a taw. He quickly went through the almost dry things until he found the old man's coat. He mumbled, "Thanks Mr. Bublings for your coat."

It was right around noon when the wind went completely wild for a few seconds, then died. There was not as much as a ripple on the water. Jodie went out of the cabin; there was a steady down fall of tinny silvers of ice. The tempter had dropped and it was colder than a Witch's Tit in the middle of December. Jodie pulled the old man's coat tight around him. "I must be right near Cap Sun

Blas." He mumbled. "Now I ought to be a moving on around the Cape to St. Vincent Island. Maybe I can catch the inside of the island and shoot straight into Turtle Cove on the backside of St. Vincent. Everybody says the island is haunted because of three pirates found lying face down on the beach with their ears and thumbs cut off. They also say they wonder the beach at night searching for their ears and thumbs. Well I am thinking, I can wait this here cold spell out and then ease my house boat into the mouth of the Apalachicola River and stay the winter." He mumbled to himself. Then laughed as he realized he was talking to himself.

Jodie untied the houseboat and pointed it toward St. Vincent Island. Everything went smoother than fresh owl poop, the first three or four hours out. Then all of a sudden, things started to get a might rough. The wind started picking up, the ice stared getting bigger, and I only thought it was cold before. My teeth were making more noise than a fat beaver's cutting trees. I pulled the old coat up until I was looking through the space between the top button and the one right below it.

Finally, the island came into sight. The current was just right it almost turned the boat sideways and shot it straight between the main land and Old St. Vincent Island. Now to catch the cove before the current shots the small boat past it.

The little old houseboat was flying.

Jodie had one chance; he worked the boat until it was scrapping the sand next to the island. As the small cove came flying at him he grabbed the long poll and ran to the island side of the boat and just at the right time he stabbed the poll into the hard sand. And with all his might, he shoved the boat crossways of the current shooting the boat straight into the cove smacking the bank of the cove with such force, Jodie found himself laying head first in the sand. He quickly jumped up and grabbed the bowline and made sure it was tied snug to a nearby, half buried tree. And none too soon either, the current grabbed the houseboat and slung it around. Jodie jumped on board and grabbed the coil of rope tied it to the stern as he leaped ashore again and headed for an old Cypress tree stump that was sticking out of the sand. He threw a loop around the stump and pulled the rope tight before tying it off.

Jodie never realized how cold he was until that very second; his feet, his hands, fingers and ears no longer had any feeling. He almost didn't make it inside. He had put wet sand and a pile of driftwood in the old tub earlier that day. And there was plenty of dry matches, but his fingers were so numb from the cold he was unable to strike them. And there was plenty of lamp oil, he placed some old newspaper under the driftwood for quick lighting, and he was barely able to take a small dipper in his teeth and dip some oil and pour on the wood. He then took a match in his teeth, struck it on the doorpost, and dropped it in the tub.

Woooosh!!

The fire sprang to life and Jodie fell across the old cot. He lay there for some time in and out of conciseness. Soon the feeling started coming back in his toes. Then his fingers, finally his whole body was stinging like he was being eaten alive by a million ants. For hours, he lay there hurting like a by-george. The wind was still blowing like a haunt when he finally passed completely out.

NEW FRIENDS

Chapter Three

It was late the following day when Jodie opened his eyes; he realized that he was wrapped from head to toe in old smelly blankets. The cabin was nice and warm. He could smell bacon cooking.

"I am not alone!" He thought. "Someone is in here with me!"

He slowly uncovered his head. An elderly man was smiling down at him. "Sorry to be intruding like this but Maw and me got caught out in this here ice storm and darn near froze to death. But the good Lord was a looking out for us. We spotted old man Bubling's riverboat, or at least we were a thinking it was. But we found you instead." Rasped out the old man as he straightened up from peering at me closely.

By now, Jodie had his right mind back, and was no longer wanting to take flight. "Mr. Bubling's has went and died. They say he got himself all liquored up and fell in the river and drowned. I don't know of any folks of his. Lest wises any that admits to it, anyways. So I done went and laid claim on all his stuff, boat and all." Stated Jodie as he struggled to loosen the blankets from around himself so he could get up and moving.

"Well I sure don't see anything wrong with that. By the way, we be the Rollins. Maw's name is Von, mines Jim. What be yours?"

Jodie thought fast. "My name is Bill, Bill Harp."

"No it ain't! Maw cut in. Your name ain't no Bill! I bees one of those Payne gals from down Bonifay way and I'm a thinking youins bees Jodie."

Jodie looked at her real close. "I thought you were one of those river gals from Holmes County, but I was a hoping you didn't recognize me. See en's I run a snag some problems and had to leave Bonifay rite fast like."

Paw spoke up, "you be talking about that stabbing a few days back? You done been cleared of all that. Old James Snips and Bill Cooley lived through the storm and showed up in Bonifay a few days ago, James done went and got him some religion. He came into town a preaching and repenting. How he done went and killed poor old Robert Willard accidental with that butcher knife. And poor Jodie was innocent."

"But the Sheriff says he's a gunna still beat you with in an inch of your life for all the problems you done went and caused him." Maw giggled, "Willard done got what he'd been a looking fer a long time, the only ones that showed up for his burial was two grave diggers and the Undertaker. It was so dat burn cold even Preacher Smith told the Undertaker to go ahead and throw dirt in his face and he would be a praying at home in front of his fireplace. Now boy you best get up and put your cloths on before all this food gets cold."

"Why did you go and take my close off fer?"

"When we came aboard we found you lying across your bed cold as ice and slap dab blue. We thought you done froze to death. Times being like they are, we thought we might be able to get us ten cent for your clothes. Maw took them off you. As she started to look around for any other loot, she rubbed your head." That's when she said, "Paw you best build a fire and warm this place up a might. I don't think this boys dead just yet." And I said, "What makes you think that?"

"The top of his head is a mite warm, she replied."

So while she wrapped you up in those old blankets I built a roaring fire. That's how we saved your life, if you know what I mean."

"I guess I was mighty lucky you folks came along when you did." I replied.

Maw smiled and said, "I think so to."

Jodie put his clothes on while still under the covers and stood up. "What's it look like outside?"

Paw replied, "don't know the doors been froze shut ever sense I brought in the last big arm load of wood."

Jodie opened the shutter on the island side, nothing but ice as far as he could see. He closed the shutter. "Mrs. Rollins I am glad you saved my life. By doing that you saved your lives as well."

She simply smiled and said, "Let's eat. And by the way you can call me Maw and him Paw, we don't do formalities, lessen we don't like you."

Maw and Paw Rollins

TREASURES UNKNOWN

Chapter Four

By the third day the ice storm was over and the sun was shining nice and warm. Maw took everything out of the cabin that was clothing and laid it all over the sandy beach so it would air out and dry.

Jodie took the old coat off and was going to wash it. But Paw walked over and squatted down beside him, "You know that before the war it is said that Red Face Pete the Pirate ran these waters, robbing every ship, boat or person he could. The tail goes that he made a good hall when THE JANIE, a shallow water side wheeler was robbed by Red Face and three other cutthroats. I kind of believe those other three lost their ears and thumbs right here on this island. There was also at one time a tail going around that Old Bubling's got over loaded on rot gut liquor and started running off at the mouth about how he robbed The Janie and buried the loot somewhere on St. Vincent Island. Before he passed out he mumbled something about a map. Thirteen days later the war started. The Blue and Gray went together like two thunder storms. At Bull Run they say they got as close as white on rice to one another. But like all things the war came to an end,

Thank God. Then the Carpetbaggers filled the South and all the old stories about Red Face had done passed from everybody's lips. So if I was you, I'd be going through that old coat before I soaked it in that there water. That map has to be somewhere. It might just be in that old coat."

Jodie looked at Jim. "Let's just say that, the map was in this old coat, how much would you want?"

"I'd help you find it and dig it up for one fifth."

"One fifth, is that all?"

"Yep, there weren't four pirates. There were five. There was one working on The Janie, a deck hand that put a rope ladder over the side. One fifth is what he agreed on. Not one cent more." Said Jim.

Jodie smiled and pulled out an old worn out slip of hide, made shiny from years of being handled. "I found the map when I first put Old Bubling's coat on. Are you sure one fifth is enough?"

"It's all I agreed on from the get go." Replied Jim.

Jodie handed Jim the map, smiled and walked away. Jim went over and sat on the side of the boat and just looked at the folded hide for some time then slowly unfolded it. In very small writing at the upper left hand corner was five names. His was right below Red Faces. "The kid knew I was a pirate all the time. But he went and gave me the map. Why? Why would he do a thing like that knowing what I once was?" Mumbled Jim scratching his head in amazement and disbelief.

Maw was frying a big pan of Red Snapper for dinner, out on the deck of the boat. The air was packed plum tight with the smell of fresh cooking fish, and little round balls of cornbread.

Jim was having a long talk with her, about the map most likely. Finally Paw walked down to the water's edge and started washing his hands. "Hey! Jodie you best get washed up, those fish is just about ready."

Jodie ran to where Jim was cleaning up. "I can't wait to dig into some of those fish. I haven't had fish of any kind for a long time. They sure are going to be good, I can tell by the smell."

Jim smiled; "well let's don't let them get cold then."

Boy! What a meal. They all had their fill with plenty left over for a snack later.

The three of them set around the inside of the cabin talking small talk. Jim asked Jodie the question that had been a working on him all day. "Jodie you knew I had at least been a pirate one time in my life. But you gave me the map. Why?"

"Look... Mr. Rollins, I have no idea how old I am. I don't even know who my parents are. Where I come from? Or did my folks throw me away? I like to tell everybody I am sixteen and my folks, the Browns were traveling to Ocala Florida on a steamer out of New Orleans, Louisiana. The first night out, we got caught in a storm and sank. I was the only survivor. But I really don't know. Now as for you Mr. Rollins you ain't no pirate. Why you helped rob that Side Wheeler I have no idea. Maybe you needed the money. But you ain't no dishonest person. How do I know this? Late last night I heard the two of you'ins talking to God. No, you wasn't talking you were more like pleading and begging him to send your three sons home from the war. You ain't seen them for over four years. Mr. Rollins, no pirate can pray like that. You both are good people. The kind I like to think my folks might have been. What say we dig up whatever old Red Face the pirate has buried and split whatever it is three ways?"

"Well I'll be son you are a mite more perceptive than I first thought." Paw gruffed as he tried to get something out of his eyes that was a watering like crazy.

Maw was a blubbering about "cleaning this dusty old cabin because it was a getting in her eyes to..."

After a hardy breakfast the next morning, Jodie and Jim bundled up against the chilly morning and stepped out into a lightly falling rain to set out looking for the three markers. It was late in the afternoon when Jim stumbled over a large flat rock. "I found one," he shouted out.

By the time they found the other two markers the light of day was well spent. And they were fast getting hungry and thirsty.

After talking it over, the two of them decided to come back later in the night and dig up whatever was buried there. In no time at all they were back inside the cabin of the boat.

Maw had a pile of fried pork and bread cooked up. I thought Paw never would get through blessing everything even spoons, forks; and knives. While everyone was eating their fill, Maw filled us in on what had happened all day. It seems a small pole boat had made at least three passes looking the cabin boat over real good.

Paw looked at Jodie, "I bet they are gonna try and board us just before daylight."

You think so, do you?"

Paw smiled; "well let's get ready for them."

"Paw you still got that old one shot pistol?"

"I sure do Maw. I got plenty of ammo for it, but no powder."

"We got us a one pound can."

"We do?"

Maw smiled, "I found it today while cleaning the cabin along with a bag of shot for that old shot gun and a can of caps.

They spent the next hour or so cleaning the old guns. Paw stuck the old pistol in his belt, "well boy I reckon we best go and dig that treasure up before those fellows come back."

"Can you shoot that thing, Paw?" Asked Jodie laughing as he looked at the gun and wondered how something so old could still fire.

"Sure I can, or at least I could at one time." said Paw smiling ear to ear.

They grabbed a ball of twine and headed for the markers. In a few minutes they had relocated the first marker. Jim stood on it, while Jodie took the end of the twine and headed for the next marker. Once he relocated it he tied off the twine. After the first and second marker was tied together Jodie headed for the third one. Then it was back to the first one, where Jim was standing. They then counted the steps between the first and second marker. "Well Jodie there's thirty two steps. What's half of thirty two?"

"I sure don't know."

Paw looked at Jodie for a long second or so, "I'll be right back." And took off in the direction of the house boat as fast as he could run.

"Where the devil are you going Jim?" Hollered Jodie as he stood there holding the string.

"Maw knows all about numbers." Jim hollered back.

In a short while Jim returned. "Sixteen is half of thirty two." He huffed as he returned.

Jim counted off sixteen steps; "right there should be plum center. Jim tied the last of the twine to the sixteen steps mark. Jodie, take this here twine and tie it to the first marker."

The two of them stopped to take a look at the map. "It says to take eight large steps straight up the middle and we'd be a standing on top of the loot." Mumbled Jim

Jodie smiled, "ain't no better time than now to find out. So let's dig us a hole in this here sand."

Well it sure looked like old Red Face knew what he was a doing. Paw made about three licks with his shovel and struck something pretty solid. He looked up from the hole, "it's a wooden box. Jim hop in the hole and help me clear away the rest of the sand. This here is the same box those three made everyone put their money and other valuables in when we took the JANIE." Jim smiled at Jodie. "Grab that rope handle and help me set it out of this hole." Jim said in a low whisper. "Now let's wait till we get this here box on the boat before we open her."

Jodie replied, "Good thinking Paw, Maw will want to see what we found as bad as we do."

They were crossing the last sand dune, when Paw said, "Listen! You hear that?"

"Hear what Paw?"

A light scrapping sound broke the silence of the night. "You mean that Paw?"

"Yaw, those swamp Rats came back a little earlier than I thought they would. Boy, you try and get behind them. I'll run ahead and warn Maw." Paw took off more like he was ten instead of sixty five.

Paw found Maw lying on her belly in the sand a little behind the boat and maybe twenty five yards up on the beach. Paw heard Maw cock the old shoot gun.

"It's me Maw!"

"Hush!" She whispered back patting the ground beside her. "Lay down here beside me; it's a good place for a shooting."

The two of them could barely make out the old wide flat bottom pole boat as it eased up behind the house boat.

The boss yelled out, "Alright get out here on deck; don't make us drag you out! Light your lanterns boys and get ready to shoot whoever comes out, what the...??," he felt his brand new 45 Long Colt slide out of its holster. He started to move....

A soft voice spoke in his ear, "to late big mouth."

And at the same time he felt something about the size of a dime and cold sticking behind his right ear. He swallowed a big lump and said, "boy is that hammer back on that gun?"

"It sure is."

"Don't touch that trigger or you'll blow my head slap dab off!"

"What's going on back there boss? One of his men asked.

Jodie yelled out, "shut up butt face!"

One of his two men, I don't know just which one whirled around and shot his boss square in the middle. Maw pulled the trigger on that there old shot gun and got one and Paw got the other one with his old one shot pistol. The deck of their old pole boat was sure in a mess, and I was in the water washing that fellow off me.

It was sure dark; Paw lit a lantern and held it above his head. "You ok boy?"

"I am not rightly sure. That fool blew that fellow all over me."

Maw spoke, "if I was you I'd be for getting out of that water Jodie."

"Whys that Maw?"

"This is the Gulf of Mexico. And there are two things that sharks dearly love."

Paw asked, "What's that Maw?"

"The Gulf of Mexico and blood, and that there boy is a swimming around in a lot of blood."

Jodie was standing about fifty yards from the water's edge, high and dry before Maw had stopped talking. Once Jodie had dried off and warmed up, the three of them went and brought the heavy box and placed it in the cabin. Jodie couldn't stand it any longer. He had to have a look in the box.

Paw took a hammer and knocked the lock off. "Jodie you found the map, you open the box."

Jodie slowly lifted the led. Everyone was holding their breath and standing on their toes waiting for the contents to be reviled. You could hear them take a deep breath when the gold and silver coins started coming into view. Once the box was opened, all they could do was stand and look, they never touched a thing. They just looked.

Finally after what felt to be an eternity, Maw suggested, "Let's put all this treasure forward and hide it real good. Paw will be a going for the law at first daylight. Those three polecats had it coming to them. But the sheriff will still have to make a report. Now, Paw, you and I have seen these men before. And the law has told us to watch them real close when they were around. So I don't think there's a going be any trouble. Jodie, when you see Paw a coming with the sheriff you high tail it to the other side of the island. We will let you know when the sheriff is gone. In the mean time we'll just leave these bodies where that are. Most likely there will be plenty of stolen goods on board that old flat boat. And Paw, if there's any reward the sheriff is a going to want part of it. Just let him take it! He's got to make a living just like the rest of us."

Jodie smiled at Paw, "yea Paw and we don't want him to stay around too long, now do we?"

Paw rubbed Jodie on the head, "boy mind your manners."

Maw stood and removed the lid off the dump hole, took a bar of soap and washed her hands, "any one for breakfast?"

Just at day break Paw took off in his small boat to fetch the sheriff. Jodie was on the beach washing his cloths, Paw yelled out as he passed by, "see you around noon."

Jodie raised his hand, "later Paw." He put his pants on wet. He looked at his ragged shirt as he put it on and thought; "one day I'll buy me new cloths."

He found the cabin nice and warm just as he hoped it would be. Maw smiled up at him, "Jodie what's the first thing you're going to buy?"

Without thinking he replied, "Shoes Maw. I don't ever remember having new shoes. Then I am a going to buy me a brand new shirt. What about you and Paw?"

"Well Jodie things got real bad around the end of the war and we had to sell the old home place. So I'm a thinking Paw and I will head back to Holmes County and try and buy the home place back. That way when our boys come home they'll have a place to hang their hats."

Maw and I had just set down to a pile of cheese and crackers when we heard Paw whistle. I grabbed me up a hunk of cheese and a hand full of crackers and headed across the island. Once out of sight I stopped and listened, I could hear Paw talking to Maw as he tied the small boat to the cabin boat. Then a gruff voice joined in, "good day Mrs. Rollins, looks like you've got some kind of mess here."

"Sheriff Pennyfellow you don't know the half of it. These polecats stalked us all day yesterday."

The sheriff was already looking the three bodies over. "Damn Jim it looks like old Thompson and those Dinging brothers tried to rob one too many! You all sure made a mess of them."

"One of these brothers accidentally shot old Thompson there with his shot gun right in the middle sheriff."

"So what your telling me Jim, is that you didn't kill Thompson one of the brothers did it."

"That's rite sheriff."

"That's too bad."

"Whys that sheriff?"

"I'll have to take the reward on Thompson myself."

Paw got all upset, "now wait just a dad burn moment there Sheriff. Any reward belongs to me and Maw."

"Only for the ones you killed. You told me out of your on mouth that you didn't kill Thompson!"

"You might just as well hush Paw, the sheriff is right."

"Well I ain't ever Maw; you mean to tell me that because we didn't blast that polecat the sheriff gets the reward on old Thompson?"

"It looks like Paw. It looks like.

The sheriff had brought two tall, slim helpers with him. "Well you boys get to polling; I won't to eat supper with Miss. Mary tonight."

"Wait up there just a moment sheriff, what about our reward?" Paw rumbled out.

"Just pick it up at my office in a couple of day." Replied the Sheriff

Paw took his foot and shoved the pole boat out into the current. Maw called out, "we'll be a seeing you sheriff."

Jodie was lying on top of a sand drift watching the sheriff as he went out of sight. He lay there for some time thinking about all that had happened since he had met the Rollins. He smiled and said to himself, "You know I think I have found someone I really like, their good people." He slowly stood and walked off in the direction of the house boat.

The rest of the day was spent just taking it easy. Finally Paw pulled the box out. "Jodie you split it up.

Jodie kind of hung his head, "Maw you do it, I ain't any good at numbers."

"Okay... Jodie, how do you want it done?"

"Why three ways Maw, one for you, one for Paw and one for me."

Maw gave Jodie two bags, "ones for your coins and ones for your jewels. Guard them close my son, everywhere you go there will always be somebody trying to take it away from you."

The Rollins left somewhere around noon. The date was December the first 1870. I remembered because that was the day I got rich. That's also the day my troubles began. The first thing I learned was if you got money just about everybody will want some of it and others want to take it all. I stayed on the island for three more days. I think it might have been a Sunday. I'm not rightly sure though. It could've been any day of the week.

Paw told me how to spot his and Maw's place. He also told me if I wanted to keep my new found riches I had best learn how to use my new Colt 45, and learn real soon. Now that I had money and all, it sure was a worrisome thing.

It took some time getting the house boat to the Apalachicola River. But I made it; here I was setting slap dab in the mouth of it trying my best to get to shore. At that moment any shore would be good! Finally with a whole lot of effort I got her headed in the right direction. And sure enough there was the run off Paw told me be watching for. Just as I spotted the runoff, I heard a shotgun blast. My first thoughts were, "Maws a collecting breakfast." But then I decided to tie off and walk in to their place. I stopped beside a huge oak tree to watch and see what was going on.

There was one young fellow a screaming "she shot me in my butt!"

And another one a screaming, "Shut up you fool and get behind a tree before she blows your fool head slap off." He was the one standing right in front of me hiding behind a tree with his back toward me, I reached down and picked me up a nice healthy limb and knocked him in the head. The other one looked up and saw Maw raising her shotgun for another shot. He lost it and ran straight at me, so I knocked him in the head to.

A Treasure…

"Hey Maw what's going on?"

"Is that you Jodie?"

"Yea."

"Watch out, there are two chicken thieves out there." Paw yelled out.

"There's two of them out here alright. And I done knocked both of them in the head."

"You hear that Maw, Jodie's done got both of them." Paw rushed over to where Jodie was standing, still holding his club. "Hey Maw it's those Smith boys! Bobbie and Jonathan and you done went and shot Bobbie square in the back side with that load of bird shot."

By the time Maw got there Paw was a helping good old Jonathan up off the ground and Bobbie was just laying there moaning. Maw looked the boys over real close. "What are you boys sneaking around here for?"

"We weren't sneaking. We were looking to buy us a chicken. We just stopped by your chicken yard to look you all's chickens over. Bobbie here bent over to look in the hen house. That's when you let him have it with that there load of shot."

Maw half grinned, "You boys ain't had a penny your whole life! And that's what it takes to get one of my chickens."

"Well Maw we were hoping that you would trade us one for a penny's worth of catfish. Ever since our Paw fell and busted his leg we ain't had nothing but catfish to eat. Now that Bobbie's done went and got himself shot in the backside, we'll be lucky to even get catfish to eat. Come on Bobbie lets be getting on home." Said Jonathan as he scrambled to try and help Bobby up off the ground."

"Now hold on there, Paw wasn't you just telling me that you would give all these chickens to somebody to tote all our belongings and put them in the boat. And that you would even throw in a two bit piece (25 cents) if they did a good job."

"You know Maw I was kind of talking on those lines. How about it, you boys want to earn all these chickens, pen and all?"

"Yes Sir, we sure do!" They said together.

"Well, Maw and I have got to move back to Holmes County and ain't got no place for chickens. So if we got us a done deal, get a toting those bundles to the boat."

Those boys got on those bundles of stuff like white on rice. Maw winked at Jodie, "we got to try and buy the old home place back."

Jodie kind of smiled; "I sure hope you and Paw can buy her back."

Paw stopped Jonathon, "now see here, you let me keep that two bit piece and I'll throw in this place cabin and all!"

" Wow!! Mr. Rollins you done went and got yourself a done deal! Hot Dogs! Wait till Maw sees what kind of swapping we been a doing. And there'll be a plenty of chicken and dumplings on my plate tonight. You just got to throw in that there coal oil lamp of yours Mr. Rollins, then it'll be a real good done deal." Said Jonathan

"It's done boy, but no more!" Paw grumped out.

"Oh boy! Maw ain't never lived in her on cabin and had her on genuine coal oil lamp before. Now she won't be a falling over stuff when she goes out at night to do her private things."

About that time Bobbie came by totting Maw's big old looking glass, "hold on there Bobbie, you know there's just not enough room in that little old boat for such things as that. So I guess I'll be a leaving it behind for Jenny, your Maw."

Big tears filled his eyes, "thanks Maw Rollins. My Maw has always talked about having one of these. But we could never get the money to buy her one. Now she can get all pretty anytime she wants to. We done got all your stuff loaded in your boat. Can I take this here looking glass to Maw right now?"

"You go right ahead Bobbie." Maw said as she patted him on the back, and claimed there was dirt in her eyes again, as she wiped them.

Maw cooked that whole pile of catfish. Once everyone got their bellies full there was plenty left. Maw wrapped me some in a clean cloth. The rest she put them in a large basket and placed them in the back of the boat.

Paw hugged me and said, "Well boy you've always got a home with us any time you want." And without looking me in the eyes took his place in the front of the boat.

Maw she just hugged me, kissed me on the forehead and said, "I'll be seeing you Jodie. Took her place in the back of the boat, looked up and smiled, we'll not say goodbye, friends like us never use that word."

Jodie took his foot and shoved the boat out into the current. He watched them till they were out of sight, they never looked back. And he knew in his heart that they would always be his family...

Maw and Paw's shack…

INTERFERING

Chapter Five

Jodie returned to the house boat. He had taken an old crate from the Rollins place. He leaned it against the cabin and was thinking about going a little further up the river the next morning just to see what he could see. "Maybe I'll stick around for a couple of days before taking off for the Suwannee River. I hear there's a trading post near Sopchoppy, just in land from Light House Point. I might just stop by there and buy me some bullets for my gun. Maybe I'll even get me a new shirt or some shoes. Could be I'll get me a pair of boots as well. Well I'll just half to wait and see, right now I had best be getting the cabin warmed up for tonight. It looks like it's a going to be a cold one."

By the time Jodie gathered enough wood for the night, dark was closing in on the tiny little house boat. Jodie checked all the lines, made sure there was no other boats nearby, and closed the door behind him.

The next morning just before good daylight he untied all the lines and caught the incoming tide. He couldn't believe how fast the current swept the small boat to the middle of the river. All he had time for was to hang on and try to steer the boat. It was turning backwards, forwards; and sideways, and it seemed like it was doing it all at the same time. This went on for what seemed like forever. Then somehow, the current shoved the boat and Jodie near the East side of the river. The swift current had carried him several miles inland. But now the boat rocked softly near shore. Jodie wasted no time polling the boat to shore and tying her off. He entered the cabin and fell across the bed totally wiped out from his fight with the river and just laid there for quite some time.

It was around noon when he stood and stretched the kinks from his back, and picked up the fish and a hand full of crackers and returned to the deck, sat down on the crate, leaned back, closed his eyes and enjoyed his meal.

The light breeze blowing off the river was cold as it whipped through his long sandy brown hair. He was watching the far shore; something was moving and caught his eyes. He strained his blue eyes flecked with gray, trying to make it out. But it disappeared be for he could make it out. He smiled; just as well it was too far away anyway. He finished the catfish and crackers. His mind drifted back to yesterday and the Smith Boys, "now that's what I call poor! But yet they were so happy and full of life, maybe no bodies told them their poor, so they just don't know better." He smiled to himself.

He leaned back on the old crate once again; he could feel his eyes getting heavy. Then he realized how cold it was. The cold was pushing its way right on into the old coat. He pulled the collar up around his ears as he made his way inside. He gathered up the last of the firewood, and built a small fire and set down and warmed his hands. Once again his eyes started getting heavy. "Wow! This can't happen, I best be gathering some fire wood before I pass out." He mumbled to himself.

He quickly left the boat and gathered a couple of arm loads and placed them beside the door. He was working on the third when somewhere off in the distance he heard what sounded like a child crying. And some one yelling four letter words with ever breath. "Not my business, I ain't even a gone a take a look. I am going to put my firewood on my boat and then I am going to go to sleep. And that's that!" He laid the arm load of wood by the cabin door, and then he heard it, the crack of a whip and the cry of a child in pain. And another bunch of four letter words. "Well maybe a look won't hurt any." He entered the cabin and poked the 45 Long Colt in his belt. Smiling as he left the cabin, "just in case I see a swamp rabbit."

It wasn't long and he was staring through the trees at two redheaded young boys. They were nine may be ten years old. One of them had a large bloody spot on his back. Jodie's blood turned cold when he saw the chains that held them to the sled loaded with wood.

"I paid damn good money for you two and I'll get my money's worth out of you and more or I'll beat you to death!" The black, hairy faced man laid his whip on the load of wood and unlocked the chains. "Now get this damn wood inside and make it darn quick!"

A tall brown stringy haired woman appeared in the door, "well you heard Jack, get that gosh darn wood in here, now!" As one of the boys passed her, she slapped him dang near down. "We paid that there government woman in Marianna ten dollars apiece for you damn boys and I'll be hanged if we're taking you back."

Jodie's mind was going wild, he was mad, and all he could see was red. At first he thought of shooting the two them and feeding them to the gators. Then he thought, "So they bought them. I'll just buy them back. No! I'll just take them!"

Jodie lay beside a tree watching; finally the last of the wood was in the house. Then the big man came out the door almost dragging the boys. He threw them in an old shed, threw in two hunks of old bread, slammed the door and locked it.

Finally darkness filled the woods. Jodie eased up behind the old shed. He spoke very softly, "you two inside, I am not one of those who are holding you here. If you will help me I will set you free. What is your answer?"

Nothing, not so much as a sound, "look I know you're in there, if you don't answer me I'll leave now!"

A weak voice, "please don't go. We will do whatever we have to. Just free us!"

The sound of a board being torn from the shed filled the air, then another, until the whole was big enough for the boys to crawl out. Two very cold boys set shivering on the ground. Jodie took off the big coat and wrapped it around them. "You boys wait right here."

Jodie reached through the opening in the shed wall and pulled out a bunch of old rags. He carried them to the corner of the house and built a fire, then knocked a window out. The big man poked his head through the opening. Jodie was squatted down just below the window. The big man felt the cold barrel of Jodie's Colt against the bottom side of his chin.

Then came the almost whispered words, "please follow us, I beg you to, because if you do, I'm going to feed you to the gators, and I will enjoy every minute of it." Then silence.

Jodie and the two boys were gone. And the old house was well on its way to burning down.

Jodie took the boys back to his flat boat, placed the boys in the cabin and untied the ropes. The tide was just turning to go out. He took his long pole and shoved the boat out into the current. At first it moved real slowly, and then like magic the outward tide grabbed the small house boat and shot it toward the open waters of the Gulf of Mexico.

Once they reached open water, Jodie headed for Light House Point. It was late in the afternoon when the first red head popped through the door.

"Howdy, my name's Jodie, who might you, be?"

The boy looked around, "hello my name's Jimmie, Jimmie Robinson."

"Well Jimmie Robinson, that there strip of land off to our right is Dog Island and off to our left is the main land. And that there thin column of smoke, well I hope that's a small fishing village named Sarrabelle. Now according to this here chart I'm a using, there's suppose to be a trading post there. So let's put ashore and find out. We'll tie off to that old tree there and walk to the village. If there is a trading post, we'll try and pick you and your brother up something warm to wrap around you till we get to the bigger trading post at Sopchoppy. There we'll pick up a few things and head across country to a place called Crawfordville then on up to Tallahassee. Now according to this here chart I been a reading that's supposed to be a mighty big town."

About that time the other boy came out of the cabin. "Hi my name is James my brother and I are twins."

Jodie smiled; "I do believe your right".

"Did you say something about Tallahassee?"

"I sure did, why?"

"Jimmie and I have kinfolks there."

"Well then we'll just have to try and find them. You boys grab yourselves one of those poles and help me get this boat a shore."

It took some doing, but after a lot of hard work the flat bottom boat was resting softly on the white sand bottom. And the three of them was stuffing themselves with cheese and crackers.

"Oh! By the way boys I ain't ever been to this place before, so this is how it has to work. We are brothers traveling to Sopchoppy where we'll meet up with our folks. Be sure that's what you tell anyone who ask." Jodie explained to the boys.

The boys found themselves looking over a few old boats lying upside down high up on the beach, several old shacks and one fairly strong looking building setting on top of tall polls. On the front of it was a sign that had a few words on it.

"Can you boys read?"

"Some." one of them answered.

"What might that say?"

"It say's Charlie's Fish Company and Trading Post."

"That's what I thought."

The Twins…

Now Jodie was a lot bigger than his age and his face had some hair growing on it and his skin was sun baked to a dark brown. And that 45 Long Colt sticking out of his belt didn't help matters at all. As they entered the Trading Post a tall older dark skin man was leaving, he stopped and was staring at the pistol hanging out of Jodie's belt, then slowly looked Jodie over real close, "you jest muster out of the Army?" he growled out.

"Yea, I did, why?" Jodie growled right back.

"Where might you'll be a heading, if I might be so bold as to ask." The stranger replied.

"Over to Sopchoppy, why might you be a asking all these questions?"

"Oh I was just wondering, as we don't get many strangers in these here parts."

"These two boys and me are brothers and were heading for Sopchoppy to meet up with our folks. And we ain't no strangers, we jest ain't never been here before. My names Jodie this here's Jimmie and that's James, what might yours be? Jodie asked.

"Folks around here call me Slim. I might have a little work for you Jodie. I'll be hanging around the boats, if you need to pick up a little money stop by and see me when you finish your dealings here." Slim said as he went on out the door.

"That was weird" Jodie mumbled as he watched Slim pass from sight.

Wow!! Jodie couldn't believe his eyes. There was everything they needed, salted pork, cheese, crackers, lard, flour, everything, even two small pocket pistols and plenty of bullets which would come in mighty handy later. The boys found coats that fit them, even shirts and breaches. They placed everything where the owner could see it. "How much do I need to pay you sir?" Jodie asked as the owner came over to the counter.

The short stocky man took a pencil and paper and wrote it all down. "That will be ten dollars and seventy five cents."

Jodie pulled out a hand full of silver coins and started looking at them. James reached over and took some of the coins, "I do declare big brother you should keep up with your glasses, you're as blind as a bat without them!" James paid Mr. Jones and thanked him.

Mr. Jones placed all their goods in three wooden boxes. The three of them was loaded down when they left the trading post. They made it to the boats on the beach and stacked their goods in a neat stack, they would have to make two trips, there was just too much for one trip.

"Okay! Here's what we will do, you boys will tote one box to the boat and bring back my box that I sit on. We will then even everything up between the three boxes. Then we will be able to get it all back to the boat." They all agreed to Jodie's idea.

"Hello!"

Jodie looked up; it was the tall man they had met at the trading post. Jodie lifted his hand. "Hello"...

"May I have a word with you?" Slim asked.

Jodie answered, "sure come on over" as he walked over and leaned up against a bright red boat.

The boys walked over also and started looking at the boats. Jodie looked at the man, "what might you want to be talking about?"

"As you can see we are real poor here and have very little money. But we done went and saved us up twenty dollars gold to pay for a little help. I thought you might be the help we were looking for. You having that there big old army gun and all." Slim nervously stated.

"Hold on there bud! I think you ought to start from the beginning." Jodie interrupted.

"Well, it all started about six months ago. This carpetbagger showed up by the name of Drago Allens, a big man and he carries one of those four barrel pistols and a big knife on his hip. Said we owed him money for squatting on his beach. Old Square Cut argued, and that carpetbagger just up and shot Squire Cut in the leg. Ever sense then he shows up and takes our money just whenever he pleases."

A roaring voice filled the air, "you running your mouth about me, Slim?"

Jodie whirled around and when he did he found the Colt in his hand and it was cocked. Well all I can say is that poor old dead Tompson was right about that trigger, when Jodie touched it that damn gun pert near jumped out of his hand. And he darn near shot that carpetbagger's leg slap dab off at the knee. Jodie was pert near scared out of his mind. He was so shocked he couldn't talk. His head was spinning like a top. He thought, "I best be saying something." He opened his mouth and screamed at the top of his voice, "These are my friends. If you ever mess with them again I'll blow both your legs slap dab off! Do you understand me; you sawed off piece of shit! Someone drag this smart ass carpetbagger off you pretty white sand!"

By the time they had put the carpetbagger on his buckboard and someone took off with him to find a doctor, Jodie was back in control of his thinking. He looked at Slim, "sir you owe me one 45 Long Colt bullet."

"What about the twenty dollars in gold?"

"I ain't earned it. One forty five long colt bullet if you please!"

Mr. Jones was so grateful for Jodie's help with the carpetbagger that he gave the boys another large smoked ham, a box of forty five longs and a case of twenty two bullets for the pocket pistols.

All the village people helped carry the supplies to the house boat and seen to it they got on their way.

ROAD BANDITS

Chapter Six

It took the boys about ten days to get to Light House Point. They found a few Indians living near the beach. Jodie sold the house boat to one of them for ten dollars. Where did Snapping Turtle get ten dollars? Jodie never asked. He then bought an old horse and wagon from another Indian by the name of Wind Jammer for the same ten dollars. The boys then loaded all their supplies in the wagon and headed for Sopchoppy.

The skies started to darken up a couple of hours before dark. They stopped the wagon and made sure their supplies wouldn't get wet. Jodie made sure the oil cloth was tied tightly around everything. By the time everything was checked, the wind was picking up and the rain was falling in big drops. The boys wrapped themselves in their blankets and were under one end of the oilcloth nice and dry. By the time the rain stopped it was dark and the twins were sound to sleep.

Jodie eased off the back of the wagon, everything seemed to be wet. Finally he found some dry branches under a large oak tree and to his surprise the ground was pert near dry. So he built a small fire and spread his blanket near it. Jodie was going to stay awake and watch after things, he was just going to lie down and relax. The next thing he heard was the twins up moving around. One of them was gathering fire wood and the other one was slicing ham. The smell of frying ham brought Jodie around. They were eating fry bread and ham, washing it down with black coffee.

Then clear as a bell, "Hello in the camp, mind if I join you?"

Jodie answered, "not at all. And welcome."

It was a fellow named Bill Backsfurd. It seems Mr. Backsfurd was a looking for some traveling company, to ride alone with till they reached Crawfordville, there he and his family was a joining up with some other wagons and heading west. Now according to Mr. Backsfurd, a gang of road bandits was a working the road between Sopchoppy and Crawfordville, robbing everything and everyone that passes by.

Jodie told the man "we could always use good company."

So it was agreed that they would travel to Crawfordville with Bill and his family. Jodie told him "we'll be pulling out in half an hour."

In about ten minutes Bill came pulling up with a brand new covered wagon being pulled by four young mules. His wife had a brand new Greener double barrel twelve gauge shot gun lying across her lap. We found out later her name was Williemay. They have three sons, Jay, Stanley; and Paul, they each had their own repeaters, and we found out later that they were all crack shots.

On our way to Crawfordville a wagon load of drunken Indians joined our little group. And every Indian had some kind of gun.

If there was any road bandit, they must have taken one look at us and ran the other way, because they sure left us alone.

It was late in the afternoon the following day when we arrived in Crawfordville. Sure enough, there were five wagons all lined up and awaiting for the Backsfurds to join them.

The Indians kept going: it seems they were headed for some sort of Powwow on up north at Lake Talquin.

I and my new found brothers found ourselves alone once again.

On their way through Crawfordville, James read a sign that said "Fresh eggs and butter from the farm to you." When Jodie heard that, he stopped the wagon slap dab in the middle of the road. Some fellow behind us went to yelling "get that piece of junk out of my way!" Jimmie stood up and spat, "Now see here Big Boss Man, my big brother is just learning how to drive our fine animal. Now you have hurt his feelings. So if you call us one more name we are going to drag you off that wagon seat and hook another Jackass to this wagon."

Jodie eased the wagon out of the middle of the road. All three boys off loaded, Jodie placed his hand on Jimmie's shoulder, "that was nicely put. Just don't let a bull dog's mouth over load a tweedy bird's butt."

The three of them had a good laugh, as they turned off towards the fresh eggs. They bought three dozen eggs, a pound of butter and a jug of honey, and got back on their way.

Once out of town they traveled about three miles and made camp for the night. Jodie built a fire and Jimmie scrambled a bunch of eggs and fried up some salted pork. James walked up to Jodie; "you know we'll most likely have company before daylight."

"Yaw, I seen how that woman looked at me when I handed her that five dollar gold piece to pay for our goods. No matter, we'll be ready for whoever might show up."

After the three of them had finished their meal, they laid out their beds under the wagon. Only this time they placed logs under their blankets. They each made sure their weapons were ready and loaded. By now the three of them were good shots. They each grabbed a blanket and eased off a short distance from the wagon, with Jodie in the lead. Jodie held up his hand, "this looks like a good place to get a good night's rest." They each picked out a spot that had cover with a good view of the wagon.

The brothers were sound asleep. Way off in the distance Jodie could hear someone coming. He set up and rubbed his eyes and listened, sure enough it sounded like two bulls in a China closet. He eased over and piled a few pieces of wood on the fire. Then went and touched each of the twins. "We're fixing to get company!"

Jimmie set up, looked around, "wow the fire burned all-night."

"No, Jodie whispered, I put some wood on it to light the way for whoever is coming."

It wasn't long and they heard someone whisper, "Don you go around the wagon and sneak up on them from the back side! I'll give you time to get in place, and then we'll take these polecats."

Jodie, in a real low voice said, "You two watch the one at the back of the wagon, don't shoot him! I'll take care of the one standing there."

Just about the time the man yelled out, "come out from under that there wagon you blasted varmints!"

Jodie spoke in his ear, "okay."

The man dropped his old mussel loader and screamed like a Banshee, "Don't kill us we're the Law!" The other law man dropped his old shot gun and ran flat out into a large pine tree, knocking himself out cold.

While the twins were taking care of the fellow that ran into the tree, Jodie was trying to calm down the sheriff. "Easy there we ain't a going to harm you or your deputy. We are just a traveling through these parts. We ain't done anything. What you trying to sneak up on us for?"

"Miss Doolittle said a gang of robbers came in to her store with a handful of gold coins." The Sheriff stammered.

"Sheriff, a five dollar gold coin ain't no handful. And that's all I had in my hand!" Jodie answered laughing.

By now Don was a getting over running into the pine tree. "Damn Johnny that boy ain't had no handful of gold. Why I was a standing right beside him and all I seen was a five dollar gold piece. Here you done dragged me way off out here through these panther infested swamps cause that love sick fickle cow done went and lied to you."

"I'm sorry Don I'll make it up to you. I'll just let you be sheriff for a week. Okay? And I'll even let you carry your old double barrel twelve gauge shot gun. Do we have us a deal?"

"Johnny you done made yourself a good deal!"

The two boys were cooking up some fried bread and slabs of ham, "you law men care to have some breakfast before you head back to town?"

The sheriff looked up; "I guess you boys done talked us into it."

We had been traveling five days, five very long days, starting before daylight and traveling till well after dark. And still no Tallahassee. We must have had a thousand little things, go wrong. The boys and I was beginning to think we had missed Tallahassee all together. Then we came across a sign at a fork in the trail, James read it out loud, "Tallahassee 6 miles."

We decided not to go into town till the next morning. Then the first place we'd head for was the newspaper office. If the boys had any kin living around these parts the newspaper would know of them.

The three of us was standing in front of The Early Morning Newspaper Office when it opened up the next morning.

A man walked up with a large ring of keys in his hand, stopped, took a long look at the twins and said, you boys from Ireland?

James smiled, "we were hoping you might be able to help us with things like that."

"You looking for kinfolks?"

"Yes Sir, we sure are!"

He then turned to Jodie, "how about you young man, what's your story?"

"I have no beginning. So I have no need for help. But my red headed brothers do, they lost their folks, now their looking for their mother's brother."

"You red headed brothers have a name for your uncle?"

Jimmie spoke up, "McDoodle, William Bonnie McDoodle."

The man smiled real big, "now that's a good name. An honest man that always pays what he owes. Lives some thirty miles up the Ocala Trail, dose a lot of trading with the Indians. Fever took his wife and daughter a few years back. You boys might want to stop by his trading post, you can't miss it. It's right beside the trail. He might just be the fellow you're looking for."

The newspaper man smiled at Jodie, "we don't get many folks with no beginning. However I do have a letter hanging in my office from a young couple who lost their baby boy. I received the letter several years back. The boy had a twin sister I think, if my mind serves me right." He stated as he scratched his head. "I don't know why I've kept it all these years, maybe for you. According to this old letter this young couple was a heading to Ocala to set up a trading post. I have no idea if they ever went, or if that's where they are still. But there's one thing for sure."

Jodie looked up, "what's that?"

"You're going that way anyway, won't hurt none to check it out. They signed the letter, but it got wet, most of their name vanished with time and it getting wet. I sure wish I could help you more. But that's all I have for you, no beginning."

"Oh by the way, my names Goodman, Willard Goodman."

The boys all shook his hand. Jodie smiled, "I'm Jodie, this is James and that there's Jimmie. And you've done a plenty, thanks."

After they left the New Paper Office they just walked around looking for a while. Jodie said, "You two carrot tops look around for as long as you like. Just remember where the wagon is parked. I'll catch up with you later. I have a little business with the bank."

Judy's Bank...

BANK BUSINESS

Chapter Seven

Jodie had never been inside a bank before, let alone put any money in one. But he had to do something with the three thousand dollars he was carrying around. He kept telling himself that sooner or later someone would find out he had it. And then they would try and take it.

He slowly looked around at the huge domed room he was standing in. He heard a young ladies voice, "Sir may I help you?"

He quickly looked around; there she was setting at a large desk not six feet away. She smiled at him and waved for him to come and see her. By now his heart was pert near beating him to death. "Everyone else gets an old man to help them, why do I have to get a pretty girl to help me. I ain't never even talked to a pretty girl before and here's one that's going to help me." Jodie mumbled under his breath.

By the time he got to the desk his mouth was dry as cotton. She pointed to a huge leather back chair, "Have a seat. This the first time you ever been in a bank?"

He nodded his head indicating yes.

"I thought it might be. She stood, I'll be right back. When she returned she had two large glasses of cold lemonade. She handed him a glass, here this will take the dryness out of your throat."

He quickly took a big swallow, and managed to croak out "thanks."

"I bet you never thought that you would be taken care of by a girl when you came in here. Did you? No! Well your one of the lucky ones today. My name is Judy Wetherferd. Welcome to Tallahassee's finest bank! My family owns the biggest part of it. So they have to put up with me. This desk is where I set at when I want to make all the help nerves. Now what is your name?"

"My names Jodie L. Brown miss."

She wrote it on top of the paper in front of her. She looked up; Jodie was just setting, gazing at her face. She smiled, "is there something you won't to say?"

"This bank business would be whole lots easier on me Miss Judy if we could talk a little."

She smiled; "I think I'd like that."

"This is the first bank I have ever been in. And you're the first pretty girl I have ever sat this close to. And the very first real pretty gal I ever did talk to. And the prettiest gal I ever laid my eyes on. And to be perfectly truthful with you, I have no idea what I'm doing."

"Well Mr. Brown you sure have a way with words. And a whole lot of firsts haven't you? I'll tell what we are going to do; I'll ask the questions you just answer them. Okay?"

"I think I'd like that."

"Good, where were you born at?"

"New Orleans, Louisiana."

"Where did you live before moving here?"

"Holmes County Florida."

"How much money do you wish to put in the bank?"

He kind of hung his head.

"I completely understand no need to say a word. Oh William."

"Yes Miss. Wetherferd?"

"Lay aside what you are doing and come here."

"Let me hold your money Jodie."

He looked real worried, looked around and then handed it a cross the desk to Judy.

When William arrived she said "pull up a chair and count Mr. Brown's money. And if he has any precious metal and jewels see that they are properly priced and the total sum is added to his account."

Mr. Williams nodded his head, and went to get a chair. She looked up, Jodie was handing her another bundle.

"Jewelry," he said.

She put it aside. Then she looked the pile of money over that was setting in front of her. Then said to Jodie, "your family has had this money since before the war. Is that correct Sir?"

He looked up at Judy.

"That's what you tell any that asks. And tell them nothing more. She wrote something on a piece of paper. Meet me out front of the bank after 3: PM. You will be paid for your jewelry tonight." She placed the jewelry in the top drawer of her desk. Then she replaced the coins in their bag. Mr. Williams returned with a chair. She handed him the heavy bag of coins.

Judy never took her eyes off the coins. Then she reached over and took one of the coins and handed it to Jodie. "Here's that coin you told me to watch for." She said as she placed it in Jodie's hand.

Mr. Williams looked up, "there's exactly three thousand two hundred and eighty six dollars and sixty two cents..."

She wrote it all down. The money was placed in a long wooden box and left on Judy's desk. Mr. Williams went to doing whatever he was doing. Once everything was taken care of and Jodie's money was safe in the bank, Judy shook his hand. "I'll see you for supper tonight Mr. Brown, please try not to be late." She picked up the two glasses and went through a nearby door.

Time almost came to a stop for Jodie; he walked around for awhile, and then went looking for the twins. He had no problem finding them; a circus was set up about a half mile from where their wagon was setting. There must have been seventy or eighty different animals, and they must have seen every one of them at least three times. They talked for a few minutes, and then Jodie said, "You two meet me back at the wagon in an hour. He gave each of them a two bit piece, grab you some grub."

Jodie wondered around the circus looking at the animals for a short while, and then returned to the wagon. He dropped the tail gate and pulled up an old crate to set on, laid his pistol on the tail gate and cleaned it. By the time Jodie had finished cleaning the Colt the twins had showed up. "You boys clean those pocket guns, you might need them tonight."

While the boys cleaned their pocket guns, Jodie filled them in on what went on at the bank. "Now this afternoon when I go to meet that there banker girl you two stay way back where she can't see you. But don't let me out of your sight anytime. If we go in a house or building one of you keep your eyes on the front door all the time, the other one walk around and look things over real close. I don't want anybody sneaking up on me. So look real good. Don't even pull those pocket pistols lessen you are going to use them. If you use them, you boys hightail if for the Ocala Trail, don't look back and don't wait for me. I'll catch up with you later. You got any questions? If you do, ask them now! After a while will be too late, so get it asked now."

"Tell us more about that pretty banker gal, Jodie."

"That ain't a question James."

"I know it ain't, but she sure sounds pretty."

"You know Jodie; she does sound right nice, how about telling us about her."

"Oh well, what the heck!"

It was twenty minutes after three when Jodie sat down at a table a cross from the bank. A young girl's voice rang in Jodie's ear.

"Hello, may I get you something."

"Yes, cool lemonade please. He looked over to his left; the twins were setting three tables over sipping lemonade. They never looked his way. His eyes shifted back to the bank door; there she was just coming out. A big lump formed in his throat, he mumbled, "Oh! God, she's beautiful. What on earth am I doing here? All I wanted to do was put my money in a safe place, till I could figure out what to spend it on." He smiled, and said, almost out loud, "What's wrong with you Jodie, you ain't ever had a date with any gal before. And this one is the most beautiful gal you ever seen."

Judy looked up and saw him setting drinking his lemonade, she just stood there looking at him for a few minutes. "Now that's pure backwoods if there has ever been. I wonder how old he really is. He looks to be

about my age. Well, I just as well join him. He's fixing to become one of the richest young men in Florida, if not the richest." She mumbled absently.

"Hello Jodie Brown."

"Hi there Judy Wetherferd."

About that time Mr. Williams stepped out the bank door, Judy could see a worried look cross Jodie's face. "Jodie, Mr. Williams is my bodyguard and my guardian. He will be watching over us to make sure everything goes the way it should."

She started to stand; he placed his hand on hers. "See those two red heads?"

"Yes."

"Those are my brothers. Their job is the same as Mr. Williams. So while I tell them, you tell Mr. Williams that they are on the same side."

She smiled at Jodie, "now that's a good idea."

The two of them got on a buckboard and slowly headed up Main St. until they came to Elam Street. "Take a right here on Elam Street. And tie up to that iron ring in the donkey's mouth."

"Yes missy."

Jodie looked into Judy's big bright eyes "are you sure we are in the right place?"

"Of course I'm sure. Why do you ask?"

"The ring!"

"What about the ring?"

"It's in the Donkeys nose, not his mouth."

Judy takes a deep breath, "you know Jodie your one of a kind. Here you are rich at the age of, how old are you anyway?"

"I've decided I am seventeen. And I know nothing of being rich."

"Well, anyway here you are rich at the age of seventeen. You should be looking for a trade. And you seem to be doing nothing." She looked back at Jodie.

He was still looking in her eyes. "Judy I have done many things just to stay alive. But never have I looked into such beautiful eyes before. Nor have I ever been able to talk to a pretty gal such as you before. I never had anything worth a flip until some friends and I dug up a buried treasure. Then I walked in to your bank just looking for a place to put my money so no one would try to take it away from me, until I could figure out what to spend it on. I didn't even know how much I had. Then there you were setting there asking me, may I help you? That's when I became rich, not on money. But something inside me did and is still rolling around. I know nothing about money and being rich, but I do know that I like what I feel. Now I sure hope all this makes since to you, because it sure doesn't to me."

Though Judy said nothing she thought, "Boy, for a country bumpkin he sure knows how to put his words in the right place."

A light wind moved his shirt tail exposing the pistol stuck in his belt. Even though Judy saw it, she said nothing. There was a light sound of a closing door behind them. Jodie turned like a cat; his hand was resting on the Colt. "Don't worry Jodie it's just the man we're looking for."

The elderly man rushed across the yard and eased into the buck board. "Where do we do business?"

She replied, "You will see." In a few minutes they stopped in front of the bank.

The man smiled "good choice."

Once everyone was inside the bank, there were four well armed guards waiting. Mr. Williams locked the door and placed two of the guards at the front door and two at the back door.

"Now Mr. Brown if you and Dr. O' Riley will follow Miss. Wetherferd, this transaction can get started."

Judy showed us to a small room with a large desk in the center of it with three chairs. She took her place, "please be seated gentlemen. She smiled at Dr. O' Riley, well Sir; it is time to show the color of your money."

Dr. O' Riley reached down beside his chair and lifted a large briefcase up and placed it on the desk. Judy took the Canvas bag from her desk. "Now according to this letter I am holding you are looking for six pieces of the Crown Jewels. Is this correct?"

"Yes, that is correct."

"Good! She gently empted the contents of the bag onto the center of her desk.

Dr. O' Riley just set there looking for a long moment. He then licked his lips, "my Lad I salute you. My search is over. Where would you like for your reward to be delivered?"

"No further than my banker's hand!"

Dr. O' Riley smiled, "Mr. Brown you are young, but very smart."

Judy cut in; "I believe the letter from your King said three hundred thousand dollars. Is that a correct number?"

"Correct as always Miss. Wetherferd. He opened the briefcase and slid it in front of Judy. Now may I hold the Jewels?"

"Just a few more minutes and they will be all yours." She stood and walked over and opened the door, "Mr. Williams, please come and help me."

"I'll be right there Missy." He entered and shut the door behind him.

"Please count this money."

Without a word he reopened the door, "would one of you boys hand me a chair?" He smiled at everyone and took a place beside Miss. Wetherferd and without a word started counting. It took some time but finally he said "three hundred thousand dollars."

She looked at Dr. O' Riley, "you may pick up your six pieces."

He ever so gently picked out the six larger pieces.

Judy without smiling asked, "Is that the six pieces you have been searching for?"

"Oh yes, yes indeed."

"Good, Mr. Williams please gather the rest and have them properly taken care of."

Jodie reached and took one of the necklaces, "this one is for you."

Her face turned red, she looked around. Mr. Williams winked at her; "I'll let him put it on you if you like."

"Oh for heaven sakes please do Jodie."

Dr. O' Riley cleared his throat, "excuse me Mr. Brown," he said as Jodie was fastening the necklace on Judy.

"Yes Dr. O' Riley?"

"There was a rather old coin traveling with the Jewels, would you by chance have it?"

Jodie walked over to Dr. O' Riley and stuck out his hand. When Dr. O' Riley reached out Jodie placed the coin in his hand.

The old man's eyes flooded up, "I thought it was lost forever."

Judy looked surprised; "tell us about the coin Dr. O' Riley."

"It is a gold coin given to my family by the King of the Leprechauns. King O'Tilley, it has been my family's luck for three hundred years. These Jewels belong to my Queen, Queen Rebecca. They were sent to America for safe keeping, by me.

However I ran into a bit of bad luck, they were taken from me by a pirate named Red Face. Now I must be going my Queen awaits my return. Do have a nice day."

Now what happened next I'm not allowed to talk or write about! However Judy did get a letter a few months later telling her that the Jewels had been safely returned to their rightful owner. Oh well that's a different story, let's get on with this one.

Once everything had been taken care of, Judy and I found us a good size stake with baked potatoes and plenty of fresh baked bread. It was late when we left Willie's Stake House. I couldn't help but notice Mr. Williams as he ducked into an alley when we stepped out the door. We stood there enjoying the nice breeze for a few moments. A bright yellow horse taxi trimmed in black pulled up. "You good folks need a ride?"

Judy replied; "yes."

The driver helped Judy aboard. Once we were seated the driver asks, "Where to Miss?"

"There's a wagon over near the Circus."

"I think I know just the wagon Miss. I carried a set of twins there earlier."

Jodie spoke up; "that's the place."

The taxi pulled up beside the old wagon, both stepped from the buggy. "Would you like for me to wait Miss?"

"Yes please. She looked Jodie in the eyes, come by the bank in the morning so we can get everything added to your account." She lightly kissed him on the lips; "I bet that was another first."

He replied, "It surely was Miss Judy. It surely was a first. Do I get to return it?"

"I suppose, but only a small one."

When he lightly brushed his lips on hers, she took in a deep breath and quickly returned to the taxi. Once a board, she said, "that was nice Jodie. No... That was good and nice." With that the taxi took off.

It was around nine am, when Jodie headed for the bank. As he approached the bank he stopped for a moment and looked around. The town was already filling up with working folks who had plenty to do. He watched three men just walking around picking up bits of paper that had been thrown here and there the day before. An older lady was sweeping the side walk in front of a large Dry Goods Store. A young lady was washing the tables at the cafe across from the bank. At the same time a fellow was passing by carrying a scoop a following a small cart being pulled by a Jackass. Every once in a while he would scoop up a pile of horse droppings and pitch it in the cart. Jodie thought out loud, "now there's a fellow that's really got a trade. Just look at all these good folks working hard at their trade; I think I'll keep doing mine, nothing!"

He crossed the street and entered the Wetherferd Bank. There was an older man looking the necklace over that Jodie had given Judy the night before.

"Good morning Mr. Brown. This is our Insurance agent, Mr. Peacock. He's insuring the beautiful gift you gave me last night."

Mr. Peacock removed his jeweler's glass from his eye, "Mr. Brown this is a very rare piece your mother must have wore it with great pride. I love the ruby in the center. The diamonds circled around it really sets it off. It's an older piece, but in perfect condition. Early 1700s I'd say. He picked up his notes, handed her the necklace, I will let you know in a few days Judy. Now I will leave you to take care of this young man."

"Thank you so much for stopping by John." She saw him to the door.

As she returned, she smiled at Jodie, "would you like to buy me breakfast?"

"As long as you don't eat too much." Jodie teased her.

She took him by the hand and pulled him from the chair. "I promise no more than a dozen eggs and a pound of bacon." They both had a good laugh as they left the bank.

Once they returned Judy set down in her big leather bound chair. Jodie set across from her. A wolfish grin curled at the corners of Judy's lips. "

"Good morning Mr. Brown."

Jodie replied, "good morning Miss. Wetherferd I trust you had a pleasant nights rest."

She smiled, "now that was beautifully said Jodie."

A young lady walked up and handed Judy a stack of papers. "Thank you Jo Ann. Well Jodie it looks like all that is left to do is for you to sign this pile of papers."

Jodie looked at her with a worried look. She leaned across the desk, and whispered "you don't have to worry; rich people don't have to be able to write pretty, just do the best you can." She slid a piece of paper in front of him. "This is your name in writing. Practice a few times, before we start. That's how my Grandfather learned to write his, after the first hundred or so times he got pretty good at it."

Jodie practiced for at least half an hour. It never did look pretty but just about everyone in the bank said they could read it. He wrote it twenty five more times, they all looked the same. "It looks like your there, let's try it." Judy stated.

She handed him a document. He signed it, ___*Jodie Brown*___.... She stood up, "Sir would you step right this way." She showed him to the same small room they had been in the night before.

He pulled the door closed as he entered. She grabbed him and kissed him big time. Then danced a gig all over the room shouting, "Yes! Yes! Yes! You are on your way to a much bigger world. Now pull yourself together you have a few more papers to sign."

Later that day the two of them were holding hands walking around the circus. Jodie broke the silence, "I've got to be doing some traveling tomorrow on the Ocala Trail, and the twin's uncle has a trading post a good ways east of here. Their Uncle is all they have."

"I thought they were your brothers."

"No," he then told her all about the twins, and what he had done.

Her eyes flooded with tears, "Jodie, only you would have done a thing such as that. You are hard, the scars on your face and hands tell all who see you that you have been at war most all your life. But your heart is as tinder as a blade of grass. You are truly a wonderful caring person."

They walked on a short distance, "I also have to go away this spring to collage. I have one more year of school. So we will have plenty of time to think of each other." Judy stated as they said their goodbyes later that night.

Jodie went on back to the twins and they prepared so they could leave the next morning.

The Ocala Trail was a foot or maybe a cart trail but not for wagons. They would have to sale the horse and wagon and go on foot the rest of the way.

There were a lot of folks traveling with the circus who needed a wagon. There was just one little problem, none of them had any money. Finally, a very large family of Jugglers came up with $7.50. Jodie shook the head of the family's hand, "we got us a done deal." While that family of Jugglers was a painting the wagon red, yellow, blue and green, the twins were unloading it.

Everything was placed alongside the wagon, and then they placed everything they needed in their backpacks. The rest Jodie gave to the Jugglers.

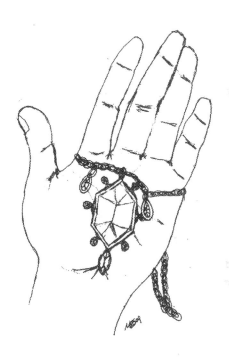

For Judy…

THE LONG WALK

Chapter Eight

The Ocala Trail began as wide as the Mississippi River, but after the first six or eight miles it was just big enough and wide enough to walk on.

All went well the first day out. There were a few people at the very beginning of the trail for the first few miles, but they became fewer and fewer until there was none. The second day it got so hot I thought we would burn up for sure. It was sometime in the late afternoon, when we made an early camp near a swift, white sandy bottom creek. I told the boys that it was most likely a run off of the Suwannee River, but of course I was only guessing. Once we checked the area out real good, making sure there was no unwanted guests, we all three went swimming in our cloths to wash the sweat out of them. After enjoying the cool water for a while we all three worked together building the camp for the soon coming night. By the time the camp was ready the first stars was just starting to show in the already dusky sky.

It had been a rough walk and a long day and in no time the boys were fast to sleep. Jodie sat quietly leaning against a large oak, his body was resting but his mind was wide awake. His pistol was in his hand across his lap, they were in no place for the whole camp to be sleeping. Along about midnight he touched James, "your time to stand watch." He whispered to him so as not to wake Jimmie.

"How long Jodie?"

"Oh a couple of hours, then wake Jimmie we want to get started real early in the morning. So tell him to shake us at four am."

Four am, sure seemed early. We filled our canteens with cool water from the creek and headed for whatever was ahead of us.

The day went by with very little rest. The only stop was at noon and the stop was only long enough to eat a few hunks of smoked ham and wash it down with water. Then we were off once again. By the time we stopped for the night we were slap dab wore out.

They made a small fire; James cooked fried bread and fried the last of the potatoes with small hunks of smoked bacon in them. While James cooked, Jimmie put on a pot of coffee. What a meal!

We had just settled down for a good night's sleep when, you guessed it, "Hello in the camp!!" Someone yelled from the dark.

Jodie yelled back, "Hello in the woods!!"

A husky voice replied, "Mind if I join you."

Jodie signaled the boys to take cover. "Not a taw, come on in, and welcome."

A heavy bearded, dark skin man stepped out of the dark into the light of the fire, "nice camp, you alone?"

"No, you see the three bed rolls, how about you, you alone?"

"Yep I am all alone."

James spoke real softly, "won't us to shoot the kid?"

Jodie turned his head so the man couldn't see the smile on his face, "how about it man with the black beard, won't us to shoot the kid? After all you're by yourself!" Jodie growled out.

"No! Wait, don't harm my baby! We were afraid you were bandits."

"Show the child on in to camp, James."

"Thank you young man for not harming my little girl, what in tar nation are you three doing way out here in this wilderness anyway?"

"We are looking for a trading post." Jimmie replied.

"Well you're about to find one sonny. About three miles further and you'll be looking her square in the face. What might you boys be looking for there?"

Jimmie replied, "We believe it belongs to our Uncle, William Bonnie McDuddle."

"You are looking for the brother of Mary Roberson?"

"Yes, Mary is our mother."

"Then hello Jimmie and James Roberson, I am your uncle. And this here's your cousin Mary Jo."

They all set up most of the night talking. The boys told their uncle just about everything. They told their uncle all about how their mother and father had died. And all about Jodie and how he had helped them escape the living hell the state had put them in. They also told in precise detail about the carpetbagger and how Jodie had almost shot his leg off at the knee. About the only thing they left out was, Jodie's money and his bank business. If Jodie wanted anyone to know about that, he could tell it himself. The next morning they broke camp early. And in less than an hour they were standing in front of a crudely made sign the read McDuddle's Trading Post. A beautiful Indian woman stepped out the door. The first thing the boys saw was the pistol that hung from her hip.

"Boy's this here's my wife Spotted Deer." His wife moved closer. "These two carrot tops are my sister's boys, they have come to live with us."

She stuck out her hand, the boys shook it. "Is your head hot?"

They smiled, "no it's just the color of our hair."

"May I touch it?" Spotted Deer asked.

"Sure." The twins chorused together laughing.

"It's just that I have never seen fire dancing on a man's head before." She felt ones head and then the other, smiled real big; "my people will love my two new sons."

Jodie laughed out loud, "what tribe is she of?"

"She is of the Cherokees." Answered William laughing.

"She seems to be very happy here."

"The Cherokee women picks her own mate, the mate dose not buy the woman."

"Is she very good with that pistol?"

Mr. McDuddle pointed at three graves under a large Oak near a beautiful creek. "Those three fools didn't think so."

"She did that?"

"Yes, my beautiful wife will protect herself and her family. She's not a person that wastes time wondering if she should shoot or not, she just shoots."

The twins had found themselves a home and they loved it. Their Uncle William gave Jodie a brand new Repeater Rifle for the kindness he had shown the twins.

Spotted Deer presented Jodie with buckskins. Jodie asked if he could spend the winter learning how to shoot, hunt and trap furs. William and Spotted Deer both agreed he could stay as long as he liked. Early the next morning the twins found Jodie near the creek building a lean-to.

"What on earth are you doing?"

"Getting ready for winter."

"Out here by the creek?"

"Yes, the air is warmer and it's nice and quiet."

Jimmie ask, "what's wrong with our room it's nice and warm and quite."

"There's nothing wrong with where you boys are it's me, I have never lived inside for as long as I can remember, it's just too crowded."

The first month Spotted Deer was teaching Jodie to speak the Cherokee language, and William was showing him all about trapping. It had become a habit in the late afternoon to build a nice size fire near Jodie's lean-to and everyone would set around drinking hot broth or some kind of tea.

Spotted Deer smiled at Jodie, "do not be alarmed early in the morning if you hear movement, my family is coming to their winter trapping camp. And you will have lots of company."

"How's that?"

"Your home is in the middle of their camp."

Jodie woke up to a family reunion; Spotted Deer's family was everywhere, babies, young boys and girls, young mothers, fathers, grandmothers, grandfathers, everyone. And by noon everyone was trying to teach Jodie to do things the right way, the Indian way.

In a week or so everything settled down and Jodie was spending a lot of his time with Spotted Deer's family learning to fish, hunt, trap and shoot Indian style.

Late one afternoon Jodie walked over to a small group of young Braves setting a round a small fire. He asked them in the Cherokee language, "What's going on?"

They all laughed, and one of them said, "Testing Limping Fox's fire water. Won't some?"

I replied in their language, "sure, why not."

Limping Fox's eyes were looking kind of strange when he handed me the crock jug. But I thought nothing of it; Limping Fox always looked a little strange, all ways going around half smiling like he knew something no one else knew. I turned the jug up and tried Limping Fox's firewater. I took three big slugs and found myself rolling around on the ground coughing, spitting and trying to breathe. All at once I set up and cried out in the Cherokee tong, "Damn! Limping Fox that stuff will kill rocks!"

He replied, "Yaw, but you and I are tougher than rocks, and we both passed out."

I woke up the next morning and crawled back to my lean-to and spent the rest of the day with my head under my blanket. About the only thing I learned was why Limping Fox goes around half smiling all the time, too much of his on firewater.

It was early the next morning when Jodie opened his eyes. Limping Fox's firewater darn near knocked his socks off. He slowly got to his feet and eased out of his lean-to. All his Indian friends had left. There was very little sign that they had ever been there. Mrs. Mcduddle was gathering eggs from what she calls her coon trap. Her coups looked pretty much like any other chicken coup, except hers had a trap. She had caught more coons and sold their hides than most trappers ever hoped to catch.

"Good morning Mrs. McDuddle did you catch any coons last night?"

She smiled and said, "Good morning Jodie; yes there are two in my trap."

"How many dose that make this winter?"

"One hounded and six, how many did you catch?"

"Seventy four," he replied.

"Breakfast will be ready in ten minutes," she said as she turned and headed for the front door.

What a breakfast, eggs, salt pork and all the pancakes and syrup we could eat. Jodie pushed his chair back from the table, "well my friends the time has come that I have to go in search of my family."

William asked, "what about your trap line?"

"I have made sure the twins know where every trap is. And I told them the traps would be theirs when I moved on."

"What about your furs?"

"They belong to the trading post, to buy more supplies."

Spotted Deer walked over and kissed Jodie on the forehead and said, "you are as the wind my son, you have to drift until you find you heart, search out your path close and it will not escape you."

With that she started cleaning the table. Mr. McDuddle asked, "When will you be leaving us?"

"First thing in the morning."

After their chores, the twins took off to run their trap line for the first time. Jodie spent most of his time washing his cloths and packing his back pack. Once all the packing was done, Jodie disassembled the lean-to cutting up the larger limbs for firewood and placing them behind the trading post.

Jodie had started for the door of the trading post when he heard a familiar voice, "hey Jodie look at this!" It was one of the twins, both of them was loaded with animals. The rest of the afternoon was spent skinning and stretching hides.

It was late by the time they set down to the late meal. After the meal was over Jodie stood, "if it is possible I would like to say goodbye tonight. I hope to be gone way before daylight in the morning." He looked at the twins; "you boys are truly my brothers and my best friends. And Mr. McDuddle, you and your wife Spotted Deer has treated me like your son. I have learned that you never say goodbye to friends, and you folks are truly that. So I'll just say until we see each other again."

With that he turned and walked out the door.

James started to flow him, Spotted Deer placed her hand on his shoulder, "he, has spoken his heart."

The Eastern sky was showing a little orange when Jodie put his backpack on and looked toward the treading post. He could just make out the three people standing in the door; it was Mary Jo and her mom and dad. As he walked toward them Mary Jo spoke, "I could not let you leave without giving you a going away gift."

He reached down and picked her up and kissed her on the forehead. "And what kind of gift do you have for your uncle Jodie?"

She handed him a skunk skin cap. "You will remember this little girl Uncle Jodie?"

"Oh yea! She really got next to me. He placed it on top of his head, reached in his shirt pocket and produced a reed whistle, and here's you a little something. He stood Mary Jo down, well my littlest best friend I must be going. But I will return someday."

He turned and walked away making sure not to look back.

The last thing he heard was, "don't forget where I am Uncle Jodie."

It's a hard thing to do telling Jodie Goodbye…

BAD TIMES AHEAD

Chapter Nine

Jodie had only traveled a short distance and already he was feeling the horrible sick feeling of being alone. For the first time in a long time Jodie was alone, and he knew it. He kept looking over his shoulder hoping to see a smiling face coming up behind him.

He had only traveled may be six miles when the wind started picking up. Huge black clouds were whirling above him. Tree limbs were breaking and falling to the ground. Jodie knew he was in trouble, bad trouble. He thought out loud, "I best be looking for shelter."

He picked up the pace, by now he was almost running; he looked off to his left that's when he spotted the giant cypress tree. It was his only hope, there was nothing else. By the time he reached the big tree the wind was blowing so heard it was tearing whole trees out of the ground and sending them flying through the air. He managed to get the tree between him and the horrible wind. It had gotten pitch dark. The only light was when the lighting would light things up. He was looking for something, anything to hang on to or tie himself to. He could feel the storm trying to pull him away from the tree, for some reason he didn't know why, but he knocked on the tree, and found it was hollow. By now he was talking to himself out loud, trying to shove away the fear. He eased his hand around to the left, nothing. Then he tried to the right, "Yes! There is a hole, how big I don't know, but a hole just the same. What if there's some kind of wild animal in it?" He smiled, "I really don't care I just want out of this damn storm."

He felt of the hole one more time, it was maybe three feet in diameter. He took off his pack held it tight in his right hand and his Repeater in his left. He then lunged around the tree shoving his pack in the hole and he followed it. He found standing room only. But at least he was out of the storm.

The storm raged all night and most of the next day. Jodie got no sleep at all, he was soaked to the bone and so hungry he thought of trying a hunk of wood. Finally the wind slowed to a stiff breeze and the rain stopped.

Even though it was night when the weather broke Jodie wasted no time getting out of that tree and getting his wet clothes off and laying them out on a pile of brush. By the time the sun light up the eastern sky, Jodie had all his belongings hanging on anything he could find. Jodie was worn slap out, he leaned against the big cypress out of the wind laid his Winchester across his lap, and with his Colt in his hand he fell asleep. He woke up about six hours later freezing.

The sky had started clouding up again. This time there was no high winds, just a stiff breeze. He quickly placed everything in his pack and headed on up the trail toward Ocala. The trail was littered with broken limbs and fallen trees which made it almost impossible to travel. Often he would have to leave the trail to find a way around a swollen stream or a huge pile of brush, which made traveling as slow as white dripping off of rice.

There was one river almost impossible to cross. It took three days just to find a place to cross it. And another day and a half just to relocate the trial again. After traveling another four days he came to a fork in the trail the left fork lead off to the north east it read Gainesville. The other forks sign read Ocala. It went off toward the east. Even though Jodie couldn't read he had seen the word Ocala enough he recognized it.

Late that night Jodie spotted a bunch of lamps and lanterns through the trees. A settlement, "it's got to be Bronson," Jodie thought to himself.

He made camp away from the Settlement till the next morning. The next morning Jodie gave the people time to start moving around before he entered the village. The storm had been devastating; most of the houses were torn apart. The people's belongings were scattered everywhere. All the people were helping each other build temporary shelter while others were gathering their belongings.

He wasted no time getting into things. He started helping the people do whatever was needed. By dark three days later everyone had a place to get out of the weather, and Jodie had made a lot more friends.

The next morning Jodie and a small group of men went hunting for meat to feed the village. They ended up with seven deer, Jodie killed five of them. Everyone started calling him "Sure shot under the Skunk Hat."

Things was starting to look pretty bad, then out of nowhere a fellow showed up with a large cart loaded with all sorts of things. Even though I was in bad need of supplies I stayed back and let the village folks do all their shopping. It was only after the last person finished their shopping did Jodie approach the cart.

"What can I sell you young fellow? I take furs just like it was money. And by the way my name is Blackie, folks all say my goods are the best and the cheapest in the whole state. You can ask anyone."

"That's what everyone is saying," Jodie replied. "I need some supplies all mine got wet, you know coffee, sugar, and salt, salt pork, smoked ham and corn meal."

"Well my good man the coffee and corn meal I don't have. But the rest I thank I can come up with."

Jodie pulled his almost empty pack off and as Blackie handed him the items he ask for, Jodie would place them in the pack. Once the pack was full Jodie asked, "How much do I owe you?"

"Well man under the skunk skin hat you owe me nothing the folks here all paid for whatever you wanted. As a matter of fact I am going to half my coffee and corn meal with you."

"Why would they do such a thing?"

"Well I don't rightly know, but they said you were Heaven sent. Said you just walked out of the woods and started helping folks do whatever needed done. Maybe that's why."

Jodie turned and looked at all the people, "goodbye my friends." And as he came he went, he simply disappeared into the woods.

By the time Jodie reached the trail it had started raining a fine mist. He wrapped a large piece of oil cloth over his head and shoulders and his pack that one of the women had given him the day before. By now the rain was coming down hard; he was hoping to find shelter. All at once a huge lightning bolt struck a large pine tree several hounded feet off to Jodie's left. He jerked his head up, the flash was gone but before it was he saw what appeared to be some type of ruin in the far distance. Right away he headed for them. By the time he had reached the outer wall the rain was pouring out of heaven like a water fall.

Then another lightning bolt, it reviled what appeared to be a, Church??? Jodie rushed through where a door had once stood. Its roof, for the most part had long since fallen in. There was a small section over and around where the door once stood. Jodie just stood looking around for a long time, then took off the oil cloth and laid his pack to one side. He was in a dry spot and he was dry also, except from his knees down. He quickly checked the things in his pack, dry, everything was dry. He pulled out his match block, gathered a pile of dry leaves and twigs, took a match from the block and drug it across a stone, nothing, he drug it once again the match exploded into a bright orange flame. The air filled with a yellowish smoke that smelt a lot like rotten eggs. The dry leaves and twigs burst into flames. Jodie started piling on larger pieces of wood, until the fire was just right. He then pulled off his high top deer skin boots and turned them upside down near the fire to dry, then lay back against the old wall and passed out.

He opened his eyes just before daylight the next morning, he dared not move. Not two feet away was a big black something, licking his skillet that he had fried pork in the night before. Finally the pail moonlight got just right. Jodie jumped up with his bowie knife in his hand and screamed before he realized it was just a dog. Laughing at himself, he watched as the poor dog almost had a heart attack; it fell all over the ground, peed all over its self then rolled over like it was dead. Jodie rekindled the fire, washed the skillet and made him some coffee in it. The dog slowly stood and walked off through the woods. Jodie smiled and said out loud, "How do you like that, it didn't even say bye."

He sipped his coffee from the skillet trying not to get a mouth full of grounds. He thought to himself "there's was no way that dog was going to run me off in all this darkness. Why there is no way I could find my way thought all those fallen trees and find that dad burn trail. And besides that I'm not willing to give up the safety of the only church I have ever footed before, not till day light, that is."

Finally the darkness gave way to a beautiful day. And Jodie got on his way. After a couple of miles the trail was clear of all brush and easy to travel. Jodie made good time for a couple of days.

When from out of nowhere he heard, "Bang!! Come out from hiding you bunch of polecats and fight us like men!!"

Then someone yelled, "You go to hell."

Jodie froze where he was standing.

Then in a low voice someone said, "Those damn road bandits has got us out numbered Jim."

"I know Mark, but we can take them with a little luck. Harley! Their trying to get around us on your left, look sharp!"

"I see him, Jim! Then another Bang! That's one that won't see the end of this here battle. Hey! Mark there's not twelve of them anymore."

"Good shot Harley, for a Rollins that is."

"Crap!!" Jodie thought why did he have to go and say Rollins for. By now Jodie's head was spinning like a top. Without second thought he dropped his pack, checked his rifle and pistol and started easing forward real slow. Finally he spotted the three Rollins boys just to the north of the trail in a clump of palmettos. He also could see the bandits; they were spread out real good. Jodie stepped from behind a large pine tree, yelled out, "you blasted Rollins don't shoot me I'm on your side" and charged straight at the bandits.

Jim jumped up, "I don't know who this fool is, but let's get in on this here charge!"

With that all three Rollins charged out of the Palmettos shouting and a yelling like a blood thirsty bunch of rebels. Jodie's first shot sent one of the bandits flying off his feet backwards. He then fired three shots real fast, another bandit went to screaming, "I'm hit Joe I'm hit!"

Another bandit fired a musket. One of the Rollins sent him to join his dead friends. By now the bandits had gotten all of this crazy bunch they wanted and took off like a bunch of Swamp Rabbits leaving their dead behind.

The Rollins boys gathered around Jodie, Harley asked, "Who the heck are you?"

"I'm a friend of your Maw and Paw."

Mark looked up, "you know our folks?"

"I sure do. That is if you boys are from Holmes County."

Jim said "let's make camp I'm starving, and besides a fellow can do a lot more talking on a full belly than he can an empty one."

It wasn't long and a fire was going and corn bread was frying along with salt pork and with all that one of the Rollins boys brought out a jar of molasses, the sweet juice from sugar cane cooked to a real thick liquid that is black in color. While they set around eating Jodie filled them in on their mom and dad. He left out all about the treasure, but told them all about their return to Holmes County; and how they were planning to buy back the old home place. He then added, "I'm sure you boys will find them waiting for you at the old home place."

They had just gathered up the bodies of the bandits and laid them out along the trail and was wondering what to do with them. One of the brothers said, "Most likely they all have reward posters on them."

Jim spoke, "I'm not a going tote no dead bodies halfway across Florida for any reward."

Mark came up with an ideal, "let's just give them to Jodie and get on our way."

Jodie spoke up in protest, "I don't won't them dead bodies, and besides what the devil would I do with them? Put them in my back pack!"

Harley's hand went up, "someone's a coming."

Everyone got deathly quiet, somewhere up the trail they could hear the soft sound of a cart coming. They quickly moved off the trail and took cover. It wasn't long and a short stocky man leading a jackass pulling a cart came into sight.

Jodie said in a very low voice, "it's ok, he's good people. But stay hidden anyway."

Blackie started whistling a merry little tune as he got near the four dead men lying beside the trail. All at once he let out a mad screeching scream and started to run blindly down the road.

"Hold on their Blackie, they ain't a going to hurt you." Jodie hollered as he ran to the man.

Blackie's eyes were as big as silver dollars, "dang boy you almost caused me to soil my cloths. Jodie isn't it?"

"Yep, come on out boys and meet the most honest peddler in the whole State of Florida. This here's the Rollins boys from over round Holmes County."

They all shock hands, as Blackie asked "you boys headed home from the war?"

"Yes sir."

"You boys kill them?" he asked pointing at the bodies.

"Yes sir."

"Do you know who they are?"

"No sir."

He walked over to the bodies, "this one is called Little Willie. This one's Billie Joe and that's his cousin Preacher Bobbie, and that one there is Slack Jaw. They all have rewards on them."

Harley was looking in the cart, "I see you have a good size ham in your cart."

"It's all I have left to trade."

"How would you like to do a little trading?"

"What you got in mind?"

"How would you like to trade that nice ham for our bandits?"

"Are you boys sure?"

"Look here we're a long ways from anywhere, we ain't about to tote those fellows on our backs. And if you trade us that ham you'll have an empty cart to hall them in." Jim stated.

"You boys load them and we got us a deal."

The Rollins boys headed west toward Tallahassee, the peddler and Jodie headed for Gainesville and Ocala.

Jodie and the peddler passed the day talking, Jodie told him his family name, or at least what he thought his family name might be. The peddler, whose name turned out to be Freddie K. Plaid, said he used to be a Lawyer from Ohio.

"A Lawyer, what on earth are you doing peddling?"

"I ran away one day and two months later I found myself in Florida, bought me this cart and became Blackie the peddler."

"You know Blackie, once a feller runs away; he just keeps on running even when no one is chasing him. I always thought it was better to stop and face a shadow than to run from it all the time."

Even though Blackie didn't reply he couldn't get what Jodie had said off his mind.

Around noon the following day they came to a fork in the trail, "well my young friend, this is where we part company." Blackie said. The two of them shook hands and went their ways.

It was a beautiful day and the night was its equal. There was nothing above Jodie's head but bright shining stars lighting up the world. He traveled way into the night, finely he spotted a large oak, he dropped his pack, leaned back against it, laid his riffle across his lap, and made sure he could get to his Colt and closed his eyes.

Somewhere way off in the distance a small child was running, laughing and playing, Jodie forced himself to wake up, to stop the dream.

There was no sound, nothing but the insects. He shook himself, maybe it was that dream. The dream that used to haunt his dreams almost every night, but he hadn't dreamed about the little girl and boy for a long time. It was always the same dream, it never changed, the little girl and her brother was always playing and having a wonderful time, then she would call out, "we have to hurry home Jodie. Daddy will be home soon and we are always there to meet him." She would always call out to the little boy, "let's race to the bridge. I bet you can't catch me."

The boy ran as fast as he could and would almost catch her in the middle of the bridge, then the same thing would happen, the boy would stumble, and fall off the bridge and the swift currents would sweep him away. But somehow in the panic of fear he grabs a log and hangs on to it, and it carries him far away. Jodie hated to dream that horrible dream it always brought great pain into his life. Even when he was in the orphanage the keeper would beat him when he would get caught crying in his sleep. He used to tell everyone he had a big sister and she was coming to get him one day. But he soon realized it was only a hand gabbing at hope, which soon vanished like a vapor of smoke. So one day he just ran away.

Jodie wiped his eyes, "tomorrow I'll be in Ocala, I hope. And maybe just maybe I'll find some answers." He made sure everything was ready for travel, placed his pack on his shoulder and headed for Ocala.

Late the following day Jodie found himself in the outer edge of Ocala. The first place he hunted for was a

steak house. When Jodie step through the door you could of heard a pen hit the floor. It might have been because the people of Ocala wasn't used to seeing a man in buckskins, hi top deer skin boot and a skunk skin hat on top of a fellow just a tad over six feet tall. And besides all that he had a Bowie knife hanging on his left side a 45 Long Colt stuck in his belt and a Henry repeater cradled in his left arm.

Jodie looked over the crowed till he spotted an empty table, walked over, laid his rifle across it and set down. A young waitress walked up and said "Sir the manager said you would have to leave."

"Bring me the largest stake you have and a pile of fried taters and a cold Sarsaparilla. And tell that boss of yours if he gives you or me anymore trouble I'll cut his ear off and make him eat it."

"Well sir I won't have to tell him, he's on his way over here with the bouncer."

"Good you go on and get me that stake and taters; I'll handle your boss and his playmate."

The big guy walked right up and said "You get your skinny butt out of here right now!"

At that very moment a young waiter was passing by, "hold up there bub." Jodie said as he passed him.

"Yes sir?"

"Look under this here table." The young man looked around then he looked under the table, "now tell this baboon what you see."

The young man stood up straight, "this man's got the biggest damn gun I have ever seen pointed straight at your belly and the hammer is back on it." Stammered the boy as he backed away slowly.

"Now fellow I just walked in from Tallahassee. I'm tired and sleepy, but most of all I'm hungry. Now here's what you're going to do, you're going to take that fat farts hand and march right out that front door."

"And if we don't?"

"If you don't, I am going to blow a hole slap dab through that fat belly of yours. Now get going!"

The big guy grabbed the fat man's hand and ran out the door.

Jodie looked up; the young girl was standing there. "Sir just how do you like your stake?"

"Well done please."

He took his time enjoying his meal. The young girl came up and asked, "Will there be anything more?"

"No thank you, how much money do you need?"

"That will be one dollar and fifteen cents."

Jodie pulled out his bag of coins, pored a few of them on the table, "could you help me out here?"

She smiled and counted out a dollar and fifteen cents, she started to put his money back in the sack. "That dollar coin is yours; pointing at a gold coin for all the kindness you've shown me."

She looked at Jodie, "those two had it coming. It just took a long time getting here."

"Maybe you can help me."

"How's that?"

"Where is the Newspaper Office?"

Major Jim D. Rollins Jr.
Calvary
C.S.A

Capt. Mark E. Rollins
Infantry
C.S.A.

Lt. Harley H. Rollins
Artillery
C.S.A.

THE REUNION

Chapter Ten

"Got here by the Tallahassee Trail did you? That's one heck of a long walk. Did you stop by the trading post at Frog Creek?" The short round face man was smiling with a welcome, come on in sort of grin. "My name is Golfer, Richard P. Golfer. And if I was a gambling man I'd bet you were wondering how I know so much about you. I even know your first name. You're Jodie and you just left the Costa Stake House."

"You sure know lots about me, how's that; seeing as I just got into town?"

Mr. Golfer chuckled; "I was behind you when you entered the steak house. I was there when you, in a strange kind of way ask those two to leave. And, that pretty young lady that brought you your food was my granddaughter, Peggy Sue. Now this Wizard has ran out of knowledge on Jodie. How may I help you?"

"I need to talk to the one in charge."

"You just did, I'm the big cheese around here."

Jodie stuck out his hand, Mr. Golfer shook it. "My name is Jodie L. Brown and I'm looking for my folks. And I need to find out if they live around here."

"Well now Mr. Brown, there's a lot of Browns in these here parts."

Jodie handed him the old letter, "this was given to me by Willard Gousman, owner of the newspaper at Tallahassee."

"Well I'll be dog gone, that's my first cousin. How's he doing?"

"He was healthy the last time I saw him."

Mr. Golfer put on his glasses, "this is a mighty old letter my boy. It's kind of hard to read." He silently read the letter over more than once. He then took out a purple lamp globe, and placed it on the lamp on his desk and closed all the window shades. Then took the letter and held it up close to the lamp. "Come, come, and take a look at this! At the very bottom of the letter where the signature should have been is the word Brown. That, I'm afraid is all that's left of the name of the person who wrote this letter. Brown, which is surely your name, now, was this letter written by your folks, only God can answer that. Now there is some Browns living in these parts and they do have a trading post. So here's what I'll do, I'll have my granddaughter do some checking around and see if they have a missing son. Now how about telling me all about that hurricane that tore the world up west of here."

Jodie told the news man everything he could remember starting from the time he left the trading post all the way to where the Rollins boys and him killed the road bandits, to include Blackie the peddler, and how they traded the dead bodies for the smoked ham.

"Well Mr. Golfer that pretty well covers everything since I left the trading post to right outside Ocala. Now I think I'll find me a room and sleep awhile. How much do I owe you?"

Mr. Golfer smiled, "by the time I get through running your story I'll be paying you."

As Jodie started out the door three young boys rushed in, each grabbed a stack of news papers and left a running. As he stepped out the door onto the brick side walk he couldn't help but think that Mr. Golfer hadn't told him everything, there was more a lot more. He looked up just in time; Peggy Sue was looking down coming straight at him. He grabbed her shoulders to keep from running over her.

She said in a very shaky voice, "Oh my!! I'm sorry I'm afraid I wasn't looking where I was going."

Jodie replied, "No harm done."

"Well Mr. Brown I see you've found my Grandfather. I do hope he was able to help you."

"Oh he did, thanks for sending me to the right place."

"It was my pleasure." She entered the news paper office and Jodie walked over to the Lily's Boarding House.

He entered the door and walked over to the desk at the bottom of the stairs. The man at the desk looked him over several times, and said, "May I help you?"

"I sure hope so; give me one of those fifteen cent rooms" Jodie said, pointing at a sign on the wall behind the desk.

"You got fifteen cents hay seed?"

Without thinking Jodie's hand moved like lighting and the clerk found a 45 Long Colt pressing against his nose. Jodie gritted his teeth, "if I ain't got fifteen cents I sure as the devil got one of these."

The man broke out in a heavy sweat. A woman's voice filled Jodie's ears, "please forgive my foolish husband's poor manners. Give this young man the key to room #4! And stop acting stupid before you get your fool head blown off."

Jodie replaced the 45 in his belt and laid fifteen cents on the desk. And picked up his key and looked at the lady, she was a very pretty woman with pleasant eyes. "Thank you Miss, now if you will point me to my room I'll get out of your hair."

"It's down that hall and on your left."

It was in the middle of the afternoon when Jodie stepped out on the street. He stood for a while looking the town over, Ocala's not very big but it's sure got a lot of people. He looked toward the newspaper office; a tall slim man was pacing back and forth in front of it. Jodie watched him for a few moments, shrugged and headed for his meeting with Mr. Golfer. When he opened the door and stepped in Mr. Golfer said, "come in boy I might have some news for you. Set down. It seems that some sixteen years ago a couple set up a trading post near what folks around here call Silver Springs. The man's name was J.L. Brown. His wife's name was Mary Lue Brown. They have a daughter named Juley Lynn Brown, who had a twin brother, that at a very young age got washed away in a flooded stream and drowned, or so everyone thought. But from what you told me before, you might just be that boy."

"Mr. Brown there's a good friend of mine standing outside by the name of Judge Tunner who wants to talk to you." He stated as he opened the door. "Come on in Judge."

The Judge came in. Jodie shook his hand. "How can I help you Sir?"

"I only have a short time and I have to be in court. So I'll make this as fast as possible. At four o'clock today I will start the trial of a young girl who is being tried for indebtedness. She is scared almost out of her mind. She just buried her folks, and has no one she knows of who will pay off her debtors. When she went to the bank to draw money there was none. She told me that she was with her father when he put four hundred dollars in the bank not two weeks ago. Her debtors are suing her for their money. If she can't come up with it she will have to work for them till it's paid off."

"How did her folks die?"

"The sheriff said a bunch of Indians killed them. She swears it was four white men in masks that did it."

"How much does she owe anyway?"

"One hundred and thirty two dollars in all." The Judge responded.

Jodie looked at the Judge, "Wow! That's a lot of money. Dose this girl have a name? Juley Lynn Brown. Jodie's lips tightened, and her folks are dead?"

"Yes, did you know them?"

Jodie didn't answer he just pulled out his bag of money, "Will you help me count out the money?"

"Oh! You can't give me the money. Be in the court room at four o'clock today, and when I ask is there anyone who will pay this woman's debt for her? You simply say I will pay this woman's debt."

The Court Room was packed. The Judge slammed his gavel down on his desk. "Shut up or get out of my court! It got deathly quiet. Not one out brake or one smart word and I'll have you thrown out, do I make myself clear?" The Judge roared.

After the room got deathly quiet the Judge addressed the room. "Now Miss. Juley Lynn Brown please come forth. A beautiful young lady slowly eased toward the judge's box. The Judge spoke very softly, don't worry young lady everything will be alright."

A great big nasty looking man jumped up and shouted out, "Yep! Tonight it'll be just fine sweet heart."

The Judge's gavel crashed down on his desk. "That will cost you Mr. Wills. One hundred and thirty two dollars and two days in jail!"

You could see the anger all over Wills face, but he kept his mouth shut for once.

The Judge asked, "Do you have the money to pay these people Miss. Brown?"

She answered, "no your Honor and hung her head blushing furiously, trying not to cry.

He then asked, "Is there anyone who will pay this woman's debts?" Everyone held their breath for what seemed forever. Then a powerful strong voice broke the silence, "I will pay my sister's debt!"

The crowd moved aside to let the tall young man in buckskins through. He slowly walked toward the young lady whom he hoped, with all his heart was his sister. He stopped beside Mr. Wills, then turned and faced him, looking the big man square in the face, he growled low in his throat and hissed "Mr. Wills you and I have some unfinished business." He then turned and continued toward the young lady.

Juley was just standing there unable to talk, trying to breath. Tears from the many years of horror and sleepless nights were flowing freely down her cheeks. Finally she blurted out, "is that really you? Is it really you Jodie?" She could only stand before him trembling and crying, a part of her that she thought had died so many years ago in the raging waters of that swollen stream, was now standing in front of her. With trembling lips she whispered, "It is you! I would know the missing piece of my world and heart anywhere."

Jodie was almost unable to talk, and then the words just flowed out like water as he gathered her in his arms and held on tightly, "the floods of time have brought me back to the bridge, so we can finish our race together, he whispered furiously. They stood that way for what seemed an eternity, as the court room went wild.

The Judge had to bring in extra men to get order. Banging his gavel he finally shut them up. Clearing his throat he continued. "Now Jodie is it?"

"Yes Sir."

"You wish to pay her debts to this town?"

"Yes Sir"

"He can't do that Judge" screamed out Mr. Wills jumping to his feet livid with anger.

"Please just give me one more outbreak Mr. Wills, so I can shoot you. Please!" growled the Judge as he reached for his pistol.

That shut Mr. Wills right up. "Now Jodie Please just give the money to the officer right over there and we will be done."

For the next two days they walked around holding hands and talking. She told him all about their folks and how they were murdered and how the sheriff lied about the Indians. With tears freely flowing down her cheeks she told how their Dad had hid her in a tiny little room under the wood pile when they heard the men coming. "Jodie they were white, and even though I couldn't see anything, I recognized the sheriff's voice. He ordered Mom and Dad's death."

Jodie kissed his sister on the forehead, held her tightly, and in a very gentle voice said, "we will take care of all this later, of that you can be positive."

Over breakfast they talked about the bank and her money. "Jodie someone in that bank across the street there stole Daddy's money. Papa did all his banking there and he always tried to keep at least three thousand dollars in his account." She kind of smiled, "he always said we're not rich but we sure as heck ain't poor either. When Poppa died the money disappeared and I became penniless." Her eyes started to mist up, "that's when you stepped out of the fog of life and all those missing parts of my life came back in place."

Jodie was looking out the small window beside their table at the large bank across the street. He could see the huge sign from where he was setting. Even though he couldn't read, he recognized the words Wetherferd's Bank. "Is that the bank that lost your money Baby?"

"That's the place where we did all our banking."

"Would you like me to show you how to find your money?"

"Do you own the bank?"

"No but I know who dose."

"Well we could sure use that money to restock our trading post, because if we don't restock we're not going to have anything to sale or trade." answered Juley.

Jodie smiled, "where's the nearest Telegraph station?"

"There's one in the lobby of the bank."

"Good, come along little sister and watch your big brother do his stuff."

"Pufftttt.. You're not my big brother, we are the same age and we were born on the same day. And on top of all that Mom said I was the first one to arrive." Juley burst out, laughing as she followed Jodie.

Jodie liked what she said, "how old are we any way?"

"We're twenty one."

"Well, us being the same age and seeing I am the only brother you have, I can be your little brother or your big brother, right?"

"Well, yes."

"Good, come on little sister."

Jodie looked the key operator square in the eyes; "Hi my name is Jodie Lee Brown and I want to send a massage."

The gray headed man pulled out a sheet of paper, "what would you like to say?"

Jodie whispered something in Juley's ear.

She whispered back in his.

He smiled at the man, "write: Attention Judy Wetherferd at the Wetherferd Bank in Tallahassee Florida." The man started to get up. "No, No, you just keep on writing. Now where was I? Oh yeah... I remember, I found my family, and it seems your bank here in Ocala Florida has lost their money and the bank needs help finding it. Please bring Mr. Williams to help find the lost money. You and I can talk about us. Yours Truly Jodie L. Brown. Now send it. And don't try faking it. My sister knows how to operate that key board."

In a few moments the massage was on its way. Jodie was looking around at the inside of the bank; to him it looked just like the one in Tallahassee. All at once the key board came alive; Juley took a pencil and paper and wrote the message that was coming in. The man just set there looking at the two of them walking out the door. He then grabbed up the paper and ran to the manager's office. Jodie and Juley walked across the street and ducked into a dry goods store and watched the bank through the window. In a few seconds a big man came out the bank door, he quickly looked around, then yelled to a man standing in front of the window they were looking through. "Hey Frank, come here and make it quick!"

They talked for a few seconds, and then the man took off like his shirt tail was on fire.

Jodie smiled at his sister, "we'll probably be hearing from those Indians that killed our folks real soon. Is there a U.S. Marshal in this here town?"

"What about the sheriff?"

"No he's one of those Indians."

"Your right little brother, we don't need the sheriff. I think we should talk to a U. S. Marshal."

Jodie just looked at her and shook his head; they both had a good laugh. "Well lead the way big sister; after all it was your idea."

She grabbed Jodie around the neck, kissed him on the cheek, "you know Bubba you make a wonderful big brother, but you should never forget who your big sister is. Now follow me to the Marshal's office." she giggled as she sashayed down the sidewalk ahead of Jodie.

Julie

THE CONFRONTATION

Chapter Eleven

Juley pointed to a small building near the edge of town. Jodie looked, "is that the Marshal's office?"

"That's it," she replied.

"It's not very big is it?"

She smiled at her brother, "neither is the Marshal, but they say he never quits tell the job is finished."

The sign over the door read U.S. Marshal Henry J. Peabody and a smaller sign on the door read, be back in a while go on in and make yourself at home. Once inside they found a fresh pot of coffee setting on a small heater in one corner and nearby was a small round table with a basket full of sweet rolls and another sign saying,

Help yourself to some coffee and sweet rolls.

In a short while the door opened and a small framed man with a handle bar mustache stepped through it .He had a forty five long Colt hanging on his hip. "Hello Juley Brown."

"Hello Marshal Peabody."

"Well who's this young man you been dragging around my town the last few days?"

"Marshal Peabody this is my brother, whom we thought to be dead until he rescued me in court the other day from an awful fate. This sir is my twin, Jodie."

The Marshal shuck his hand, "well Jodie Brown I want to thank you for what you did in that court room and how you handled big mouth Wills, who you'll probably be seeing again real soon."

"Thanks Marshal, Mr. Wills, I believe is one of the reasons we came to see you."

"You've got the wrong man; you need to talk to the sheriff."

"My sister and I believe the sheriff is one of the other reasons."

"Hold up, let's talk a spell and make sure we're all three standing on the same cow patty. Now tell me just what the buggerwitch are you two up to anyway?"

Juley filled the Marshal in on what went on at the bank. And how the bank President acted after they left the bank, how he called to Frank and talked to him and how Frank ran straight to the sheriff's office. She also told about what she had heard while she was hiding under the wood pile the night her parents were killed.

The Marshal leaned back in his big chair, "you know Juley, I've been checking around looking for who killed your folks. And I've ran in to a block wall ever which way I turned, until just now. You two just gave me the clue I've been looking for."

Jodie slid to the front of his chair, "how's that Marshal?"

"You two tied the banker and the sheriff with the same rope. I knew the sheriff lied about the Indians doing it, because I know every Indian within a hundred miles in every direction and everyone of them is my friends. And I knew that the banker had misplaced your money. But I couldn't put the sheriff and Mr. Bennet, the bank manger on the same cow paddy till you two set me straight. I am starting to think like you two. I do believe you are going to get a visit from those Indians real soon. Now here's what we are going to do, you two put the word out that you are going out to the trading post tomorrow. I'll ease on out there sometime tonight. I need to talk to some fellers between here and there that are scared of the dark."

Jodie smiled, "what's being scared of the dark got to do with you talking with them?"

"It makes them easy to find, they build big camp fires. You two take off and we'll meet up tomorrow at the trading post."

Jodie and Juley stopped by the newspaper office. Mr. Golfer was setting at his desk; "you two have a seat and let me read you tomorrow's news."

"Mr. Golfer can we talk to you first?"

"Sure what's up?"

"We are trying to smoke some polecats out of hiding, and we need some help."

"What do you want me to do?"

"We want you to write a small story in tomorrow mornings news that my sister and I are going to our trading post first thing in the morning."

"That's good, I can sure do that in these parts you two are the news."

"Now what's tomorrow's news?" Jodie asked.

"I'm running your big shoot out story again."

"Good you can add this to it; I think I recognized the road bandit's boss in Judge Tunners court room the other day."

"For real you think you recognized him." asked Mr. Golfer.

"I don't think it, I know it, but let's use the word think anyway." Jodie replied.

"My God Jodie I'll have to run this story for at least three days! There hasn't been this kind of news in years around here. I've got to get the press going this is hot stuff." replied Mr. Golfer, all excited. As the two of them left the news paper office they met Peggy Sue, "he'll sure be glad to see you Miss. Peggy."

She smiled and said, "He's always glad to see me."

The two of them went straight to the steak house. They were met by the management, "right this way Mr. Brown, Miss Brown; your waitress will be here shortly to take your order."

Juley looked up just as Peggy Sue was coming through the door. She waved and Peggy came over to their table. Juley smiled, "are you working?"

Peggy smiled back, "well I reckon."

"Good you are now our waitress."

Peggy pulled a note pad and pencil from her apron pocket; "may I take your order kind Lady?"

They gave their order, "my Sir that's a lot of food for such a skinny, tall man. Are you sure you can eat that much?"

The three of them had a good laugh, he then replied, "oh no but I'm going to be caught trying."

The sheriff was setting right behind them. Jodie was setting where he could see him. Peggy Sue turned to leave their table, "oh before I forget, please tell your Grandfather that Juley and I are going out to our trading post first thing in the morning. So we won't be keeping our ten o'clock appointment.

"Papa and I are going to work late tonight I'll sure to tell him."

Jodie watched the sheriff's face when he told Peggy about the following morning, how an evil smile came across it. The sheriff stopped eating and left the steak house in the middle of his meal. A wolfish grin came across Jodie's face.

Juley looked at him kind of puzzled, "and just what are you grinning about?"

He simply replied "massage sent, massage received, and massage left."

Peggy Sue eased up behind Jodie with their order, leaned her head over and asked "did the sheriff get the message we sent him?"

"You know I do believe he did Miss Peggy."

She placed their food in front of them, smiled at Juley, winked and said, "Your brother is just the most."

Jodie looked up with a real strange look on his face and replied, "Most of what?"

The girls had a good laugh and Peggy turned to leave.

Jodie said "wait a second Miss Peggy. Please tell the owner of this here place that I would like a word with them after we finish our meal."

"I will try Jodie sometimes they are at home. I will check their office. If they are there I will tell them. Peggy replied.

They took their time eating and planning out what and how they would handle the following day. Once they finished a waiter came and cleaned their table and brought them a cup of coffee. Peggy walked up and said, "Mr. and Mrs. McMillon, I would like you to meet Mr. Jodie L. Brown and his sister Miss. Juley Brown. Jodie, Juley, these are my boss and owners of this stake house."

The little lady smiled, "thank you Peggy."

Jodie and Juley stood and shook their hands. Juley said, "Please set down and join us."

Mr. McMillion slid his chair forward, "I understand you would like a word with us."

Jodie cleared his throat, "yes sir I would. When I came in to your cafe I saw your small sign in the corner of your window. Could you tell me what it says?"

The little lady's eyes smiled and the corners of her lips curled up at the corners. "It reads this business is for sale."

"I thought that's what it said. Now would you tell me your asking price?"

"Young man my wife and I want to go back to our place of birth in Skowhegan, Maine so we can live out the remainder of our days among our friends and love ones. We have a small house there and we have a small savings." He then smiled real big; "we are even packed and ready to go. But there's just one problem, we have to sale our home and steak house before we can go home. So our asking price for our home and steak house is three thousand dollars."

Jodie looked at his sister, "is that a lot of money Baby girl?"

"Jodie that's a lot of money for poor folks, but it is very little for someone who has plenty."

"So what you are telling me Little Sister is, it's a good deal for someone who has three thousand dollars."

"Yes it's a real good deal for someone who has the money." Laughed Juley.

Jodie, without taking his eyes off his sister said, "Sir do you have something to write with?"

Mr. McMillion replied, "Yes of course," he looked up and waved to Peggy Sue.

She walked over to their table, "yes sir."

"Please go to my office and bring paper and ink."

In a few seconds she returned with writing material. Jodie looked up, "Drag you up a chair Miss. Peggy; I need you to write some words for me."

"Yes Sir Mr. Brown. What would you like me to write?"

"Hi Judy this here's Jodie, I want to buy this here Stake house. Please have Mr. Williams, take care of it for me. Signed <u>MR. Jodie L. Brown</u> ."

Peggy smiled at Jodie, "is that all you wish to say Jodie?"

Juley cleared her throat, "just add I've been a missing you a lots."

Jodie's eyes sparkled with approval.

She handed him the paper and said, "that's nicely said Jodie."

He folded the letter and handed it to Mr. McMillion, "in a few days a beautiful young lady will be coming through that door a looking for Jodie. Her name is Judy Wetherferd. If I ain't back by the time she gets here give her this here letter. She will see that you get paid."

With that Jodie and his sister got up and headed for the boarding house.

The sun was just starting to light up the streets, when the two of them started for the stables the following morning. The sidewalks were already full of people hurriedly going about their chores. Just about everyone knew them by sight if not by name. Almost everyone they passed, either nodded, spoke or shook their hands. It seemed like it was going to take forever for the black smith to hook up their wagon, so they could get started. Jodie said later that the black smith "could probably talk the horns off a billy goat."

Peggy Sue waved as they passed the newspaper office. The safest route was by way of Fort McCoy so they headed north east. It was midday when they reached the Fort. Juley pointed to a well used road headed straight south and said, "about a half mile down that road is the salt mine, we best pick up four barrels of crushed salt, we're out at the trading post. And salt is our best seller."

Jodie looked at his sister, "what do we need so much salt for?"

She laughed and said, "Cooking, curing skins, and the Indian's buy it for trading further south."

Jodie had no problem spotting the salt mine as he stopped the wagon in front of a big old shack. He jumped down and helped his sister down. A tall skinny man came out of the shed, "Hello, Miss. Juley my wife and I was right sorry to hear about your folks."

She thanked him and said "Mr. Smith this here's my brother Jodie."

He smiled real big and said, "So we've all heard in these parts. He shook Jodie's hand, what can I do for you Mr. Jodie?"

"We need four barrels of crushed salt."

Without so much as a move of his eyes Mr. Smith said, "Joe you and Tom load four barrels of that crushed salt on Miss. Juley's wagon."

Jodie turned to see who Mr. Smith was talking to. He found himself facing two of the biggest men he had ever seen. They just walked over and grabbed a barrel of that salt and set it on that wagon like it was full of feathers and loaded the other three the same way.

He looked at Juley, "did they just do what I think they did?"

She smiled and said "Thanks Tom. Thanks Joe" and reached in her small hand bag and brought out two dimes giving each of them one.

Once they paid for their salt they headed straight south for Silver Springs and the trading post, arriving there around ten o'clock that night. Jodie stepped down from the wagon and was helping his sister down. "If that's salt in those barrels you best move them to one side and cover them with oil cloth, it looks like rain." came a gravelly voice from the pitch black night.

"Damn you marshal you just scared the bygiggers out of me."

"Didn't scare Missy none, she seen me coming. Missy I've been here all the day and most the night I sure could use a cup of coffee." Laughed the Marshall as he sat down.

She smiled; "I'll put a pot on right away."

In a few moments the kitchen light up, "Jodie you and the marshal bring in some firewood and don't forget the kindling."

Jodie and the marshal set around an old well used table sipping hot black coffee going over every possible thing they could think of that they could use to overcome almost impossible odds. Juley brought the coffee pot around, the marshal sled his cup to one side for a refill and said, "you know we are a going to be bad outnumbered tomorrow when they come, so we best get them in a crossfire and cut their numbers down real fast like. You know get as many of them as we can real fast." Then he laughed and said, "I am going to shoot that blasted crooked sheriff right through the ankle, that is if he has guts enough to show up. He's the kind of cowered that sends someone else to do his fighting. But, it really doesn't matter none I'm still a going walk his horse right out from under him and watch him kick his boots slap dab off. I've got plenty of proof that he was in on killing your folks along with a half dozen others and I've got everyone of their names. Yes sir, that's a going to be some kind of hanging."

Juley looked at the marshal with tears in her eyes, "but why would they kill our folks, they were just hard working; honest, and church going people?"

"Well girl it seems that there's a going to be one of those big roads a going to come through here and their paying big money for the land."

"But what does that have to do with us?"

"Well darling your land is setting slap dab in the middle of their road and your Paw wouldn't sell. So that banker fellow got with the sheriff and killed your folks and stole your money and was a going to enslave you. But your brother showed up and spoiled their plans."

"Where dose Wills fit in?"

"Well boy he claims your Paw borrowed money from him and has a paper with you paw's name on it showing where he borrowed the money. So he'll most likely be here in the morning. But if he's not, it won't matter none, he's one of those poor bastards I'm a going hang. That is if there are any of them left after the shoot out in the morning. Judge Turner and I are a going to gather them all up and he's a going to convict them and I'm a going to hang them. On my way here yesterday I found those boys that I told you about,

you know the ones that are scared of the dark. Well anyway, I told them I would give them fifty cents each if they would show up for the shooting. They wanted a little more so I agreed to throw in a case of bullets, but only if they used some of them on those white Indians. They all liked that idea and said they'd be here just before daylight."

Jodie looked at the marshal, "what makes you think they will show?"

The marshal pointed at Juley, "Because she is the only friend they claim, she is one of them as far as they are concerned. And they will die for one of their own."

Juley walked over and placed her hands on Jodie's shoulders, "you're talking about the Cone Family aren't you?"

"Yes I am Missy."

"They're not afraid of a fight," she replied.

With that the marshal stood up and said, "we best be getting ready for them, pack that stove slap full of wood we want them to see lots of smoke coming out of that stove pipe when they get here. We want them to think that you two are all alone and a sleep. That way they will come charging straight into hell, that's when we will thin them out. Now you two grab you some blankets and camp out in the smoke house and be ready for them. You'll most likely hear them coming a long time before you see them. Now let's do what we have to and get it over with."

Once the two of them got settled down in the smoke house Jodie asked, "who is the Cone's?"

"They are the last of the nomads, they stay on the move, and they never stay in one place very long. They live off the land and call no place home."

"How is it you know them so well?"

"They were here when we arrived in this part of the country. Papa was building the trading post when one day four men showed up caring a woman on a make shift litter, she was bad sick. Mama and Papa went out to meet them, they asked for help. They put her in our tent and Mama started treating her. By late afternoon the whole area was full of Cones. In a couple of weeks Mama Cone was a lot better. While they were here, they kept us plenty of meat and fish and helped Papa build the trading post. Ever since then they have showed up to trade for salt, flour and lard," she yawned and said in a very tired voice, "and there was hardly a day passed that one of the Cones didn't at least walk by this place. They sure loved Mama and Papa." With that she snuggled up close to her twin brother and went fast to sleep.

It was starting to rain and the wind was picking up a little. Jodie made sure the blanket was wrapped good around his sister. The wind was blowing the damp air through the cracks between the boards of the walls. The last thing Jodie remembered was looking up and thinking, "thank God the roof isn't leaking."

Somewhere in the depth of his mind there was a sound, a twig snapped or was it the wind? Jodie's eyes slowly opened. His hand was resting on the 45 long Colt. He lay there for a long while just listening to the night. It had quit raining; he could see the stars shining through the cracks. It was somewhere around four in the morning. Jodie touched his sister's shoulder; "we'll be getting company real soon."

She replied, "good morning little brother."

Jodie started to say something but was cut off by a very young voice, "I'm right sorry about that there twig Miss. Juley."

She quickly looked at Jodie with a surprised look, then with a light smile and said, "James is

that you?"

"Yes, Miss. Juley. Paw told me to come and look after you. The rest of the family is a scattered out along the road, we're going to let those varmints in but they won't be a leaving."

"Well come on in here and meet my brother, James." Juley whispered back.

In a few moments the barrel of a fifty caliber mussel loader came easing through the door and attached to the other end was a black headed tall skinny boy around eleven years old.

"James, this here's my brother Jodie."

"Is he the one the Lord took away?"

"Yes, but the Lord gave him back."

"Well praise the Lord Miss. Juley, I ain't never met nobody that the Lord has given back before. Can I touch him? You know, him being a ghost and all, all my kin folks say you can't touch a ghost, your hand will just pass right through them."

Jodie smiled and said, "You can touch me I'm not a real ghost."

"My kin said you ghost would try and fool me by saying you're not a real ghost." James replied as he scooted back a few feet.

Juley could see that James was getting worried, so she put her arms around Jodie's neck and hugged him.

"James he's my brother not a ghost."

James smiled and said "you had me going there for a mite. He stuck out his hand, I'm right proud to make you're acquaintance."

Jodie shook his hand, "I'm sure glad to meet you to James. Jodie looked at the riffle the young boy was holding; it was a good six inches taller than him. That's a mighty big gun you got there ever shoot it?"

"Yes sir Mr. Jodie folks around these parts all call me Bear Slayer."

"Why is that?"

"Cause I hunt Bears."

"You ever get any?"

"Three last year and six so far this year."

"That's some kind of shooting."

"Mr. Jodie we best be for getting ready."

"Why's that James?"

"Because there's a bunch of riders coming hell bent for leather straight at us." Replied James with a grin the size of Texas on his face.

Jodie smiled back at the boy, "I think your right. I do believe we're about to get company." He looked at his sister, "Juley the Lord gave us those pine trees for many reasons one of them was to hide behind. Please use them."

"Don't you be a worrying about me and get yourself hurt. Papa taught me to shoot well with a long gun, can I use yours?"

As Jodie handed her his riffle he gave her a weak smile and said "shoot straight baby sister you all I've got."

He then eased out the smoke house and moved off to his left, closer to the trading post. The trading post was now between him and the marshal. He knew that he and the marshal would be charging straight at the raiders with little cover. He was thinking to himself as he checked his six shooter, "every bullet has to count". He placed six extra bullets in his shirt pocket he could always reload a lot faster when he had his extras in his shirt pocket.

The marshal was on the other side of the trading post standing in the shadow of a large pine with a six shooter in each hand; he also knew what had to be done. The sound of beating hooves was now ringing in everyone's ears, the sound of men screaming like wild Indians charging straight at the Marshal and Jodie thinking it was going to be easy, not knowing what was awaiting them.

Jodie could feel his hands starting to sweat, he could taste the copper in his mouth, as he seen the first rider come into sight; the others close behind. Then quietness for what seemed like forever. He felt the Colt jump into his hand and saw the rider go flying backwards off his horse.

Juley was watching her brother, as he made his stand, she saw him as he started to reload, she saw as he spun around from the impact of a bullet hitting him in the side, and in what seemed like the same movement how he whirled back facing the enemy still reloading. Then as a charging rider bore down on him and he knew he had no chance of escape.

Then the sound of a cannon exploding beside her made her jump almost out of her skin, and the horse and its rider piled up at Jodie's feet. James had dropped the hammer on that big gun. She quickly looked; he was reloading for another shot. She turned back to face the battle just in time to see the Marshal almost go down.

She fired the repeater and the rider nearest the Marshal went flying from his saddle. Juley saw a tall slim shadow step out of the woods and fire a musket, it was old man Cone himself. Then the whole Cone family just ghosted in, and joined in the fray. The fight was on. Jodie and the marshal were charging head first into the battle. She and James watched as Jodie and the marshal stopped and took aim. They saw two more riders charging straight at Jodie and the Marshall. It was the sheriff and Mr. Wills.

The marshal fired first hitting the sheriff through the ankle. Then Jodie fired, ending all of Mr. Will's problems. The battle was over as fast as it started, or so it seemed.

The Cone family was gathering up all the weapons and placed them on the old wooden table inside the trading post; while the Marshal had the raiders that weren't all shot up unload the barrels of salt off the wagon

and load their dead and wounded on it. The Marshal then had four of the Cone boys hogtie the healthy ones and load them on the back of the wagon.

Just as he started to place a guard on the prisoners Juley spoke up, "let me pick the guard."

"You go right ahead Missy."

"Marshal, this here's my very good friend James Eugene Kap Cone. And I think he's old enough and big enough to stand guard over these white Indians." That's what they were called for many years to come. "Oh! And by the way fellers, Mr. James is better known as Bear Slayer around these here parts."

One of the bad men mumbled, "I ain't scared of no kid, even if he does have a big gun!"

"If any of you have any doubts as to whether he can shoot that fifty cal. or not, have a look at that man's head lying on top of the pile. He made that shot at over a hundred and fifty yards." Juley stated.

James never smiled he just looked at the men on the wagon, pointed the barrel of his long gun at them, turned and walked off about 25 yards set on a stump and laid his gun across his lap.

The only Cone that went inside with Jodie, Juley and the Marshal was Mr. Johnnie Down Wind Cone. The Old Coon skinner himself, head of all the Cone family, he walked over and stood beside Juley, "what you reckon the Marshal is a going to do with all those nice long guns."

She smiled and said, "Let me ask him, Marshal what are you going to do with this pile of guns?"

He replied, "I'm not rightly sure, you got any ideas?"

"No, but Papa Cone might have."

The marshal wanted to smile but kept a sober face, "what you thinking Mr. Cone?"

"Well I been a thinking, us Cones could sure use us some nice long guns. And there was neigh on fifteen of us did some shooting. That's a lot of fifty cent pieces. So if you want to trade all those long guns and their bullets for all those fifty cent pieces we're willing."

"What about the hand guns?"

"We Cones don't need any hand guns. We do all our shooting from a far. So you keep them."

"Well Mr. Coon Skinner we got us a done deal." The two of them shook hands on it.

The old man walked to the door and whistled, a dozen or so big young boys came a running. "Come on in here boys and get these long guns and bullets. Leave the hand guns where they are."

"What you want us to do with them Papa?"

"Take them to Maw."

Mr. Cone started to leave behind the boys; Juley hugged him and said in a soft voice, "thanks Papa Cone for all your help."

A tear ran down his cheek, "we're family, those varmints did great harm to this family. They had to pay." With that he joined his family.

Juley picked out a young mare from the bandits horses, took the saddle off and rubbed it down real good, saddled it, looked at Jodie, "I'll head for town and send the doctor out to meet you and the Marshal. Some of those bandits are in pretty bad shape."

Before Jodie could protest she was headed for Ocala. The Marshal grinned at Jodie, "she's a lot like your mom and a little like your dad."

"You knew my folks real good Marshal?"

"I've ate a many a meal with your folks boy. This is one place I was always welcome no matter what time day or night. Your maw always had a pot of coffee on the stove and a wafer of biscuits in the oven. Yaw! I'd say I knew your paw real good. We skinned a many a gator and our share of coons together. Your paw was the only true friend I ever had. Now boy we best be getting this bunch to town, before some of them get over ripe."

"Well Henry I reckon your right. I think I'll hire James to ride along on the wagon with me. That is if his folks don't mind."

James talked it over with his folks and climbed on the wagon, grinned up at Jodie, "heck fire Mr. Jodie you don't have to pay me nothing. I never have been to no town before, so that's payment enough."

It was near noon when the Marshal headed toward town with Jodie following close behind with the wagon.

The sun was high as they traveled the rutted road; it was not easy to follow. The horses were just breaking a good sweat, when the marshal called a halt. "We'll let the horses rest a while, you two get down from that wagon seat and stretch your legs, it's still a long haul to Ocala."

They rested for an hour or so and headed out once more for Ocala. They had been on the move for several very long hot hours and the sun was beginning to set. The marshal was riding alongside the wagon talking to Jodie; James reached over and touched Jodie on the shoulder, "there's a rider a coming mighty fast and headed straight for us."

"Hold up Jodie, I'll ease off to the side and we'll find out who's in such an all fired hurry," the Marshall said as he cut to the side of the road into the brush.

It turned out to be the doctor. "Miss. Brown told me you were headed to town with some wounded, but this is ridicules. What the sam hell happened out here, another Bull Run? Miss. Brown said there had been some shooting but she didn't say anything about a war." He panted as he leaned on his saddle horn and looked over the wagon at the bodies.

While the doctor patched up the wounded the Marshal and Jodie got some rest. James said he had rested well on the wagon seat so he would keep watch...

It was full daylight the next morning, when the worn out group stopped in front of the sheriff's office. The Marshal stepped down from his horse stretched and looked around, "there sure seems to be a power full lot of people in town today. Where do you reckon they all came from?"

"I'd say my little sister done a good job of putting the word out about what happened at Silver Springs." Replied Jodie wiping sweat off his face. "Great heavens to betsy but it's hot out here today."

It seemed the whole world knew about the big shoot out at Silver Springs. People were pouring into Ocala from everywhere, Pensacola Florida, Mobile Alabama; and Birmingham Alabama, Macon Georgia; one couple even came all the way from Chattanooga Tennessee. The Flying Horse Stage was just unloading from Jacksonville, Florida when Jodie and James hopped down from the wagon. It had been a hard three days coming from the trading post; as he looked at all the people, Jodie said "I'll say it again; I think my big sis did really good putting the word out."

The marshal chuckled as he stepped up on the wooden walk, "I would reckon so."

All the people looked up and saw the wagon and started running for it. Some of them had pencils and writing pads, news paper people. Some had cameras but most just wanted to see the notorious road bandit Jessie Will's body. The marshal stepped in front of the mob.

Bam! Bam! Bam! He fired his six shooter, the mob came to a stop, "listen up I am U.S. Marshal Henry J. Peabody and I'll shoot the first one that gets close to this here wagon! Now back off, you'll have plenty of time later to look, ask questions and even take pictures. Now find some place other than here to hang out!"

About that time Mrs. Wilder, the Undertakers wife walked up, "want me to take my part of these varmints, marshal?"

"Yaw! Clean them up; I'm sure the sheriff knows their names and all. I'll bring him around later so we can find out who they are. I'll let you know when to display them."

She replied, "Best make it sooner than later, their already getting pretty rank."

"Oh hell! Annie Lue, soak them in a vat toilet water for a while and have a showing first thing in the morning." He answered her. The marshal watched as the undertaker's wagon eased off down the street. "Well let's get the rest of this bunch inside before more of them die out here in this dad burn heat..."

Once they were inside and locked up, the Doctor looked the wounded over once again. The doctor smiled at Jodie, "you know if I was you I'd be for taking a walk over to the steak house I do believe I seen a mighty pretty Gal that I ain't seen in a long time going in there a while ago."

Jodie smiled as he shot out the door and all but ran to the steak house door. Then stopped, he could see inside, Juley was facing the door, Judy's back was toward him. A large lump formed in his throat. He wanted to break out in tears of joy but dared not do that. "She really came all the way to Ocala because I ask her to?" His thoughts were running wild. "What will she do when she sees me? Do I embrace her or shake her hand?" His heart was all most jumping out of his chest. He had no idea what his hand was doing opening the door. "What is my feet doing walking toward her? Is my mouth going to work when I get to her?" All he could think to himself was, "Hi... I love you. And will you marry me? Please don't say no!"

She whirled around as he stammered out, "I've missed you so much and I love you."

Before he could say another word she was in his arms and simply said "I love you also, and I've also
missed you a heck of a lot."

"Will you marry me Judy, I mean I am just a back water hick, but I will love you forever and a day, if you will have that is..." Jodie asked as he held her closer still.

"Yes! Yes! I don't care about anything to do with where you are from or how you got here. I just know you have become my heart beat... My world..." Answered Judy through tears of sheer joy.

Mr. Williams was setting at a nearby table, jumped up and shouted out, "Yes, she did it, she did it, yes, she did it. Thank God my niece landed her a good man! That has no idea what a lot of money is and doesn't really care. But has a hell of a lot of love for my little girl." Then he just stood there and danced in place.

All Juley could do was set down and cry and clap her hands. Peggy Sue sat down beside her and did the same.

Once everything settled down Jodie looked at Peggy, "is there anyone who can be trusted to guard the prisoners?"

"There are a lot of good people here in town, but the best man for the job would be our ex-sheriff, Mr. Longberry. He's honest and trustworthy and he puts up with no foolishness."

"Just how do I find this Mr. Longberry?

A very strong voice filled the air, "just look behind you young man."

Jodie turned and found himself looking in the eyes of a short stocky clean shaven man with gray hair and a scare across his left cheek. He reached out and shook Jodie's hand. "Hi my names Coronal James R. Longberry and I'd be pleased to help Henry any way I can. Is he at the jail?"

"Yes Sir."

"Oh by the way Mr. Brown you might want to have somebody look at that bullet hole in your side. That pretty gal pert near squeezed you in half." He tipped his hat and headed for the jail.

In all the excitement Jodie had forgotten all about the wound in his right side. He looked down; his buckskins were socked with blood all the way down to his ankle. He smiled weakly, "Miss. Peggy the marshal got hit also, please check on him." He then looked around and almost buckled at the knees. "You know, I think I had best lay down somewhere."

Mr. Williams held him on his feet, "where do you won't him Miss. Juley?"

"Lilley's Boarding House would be the best place."

As they walked through the front door of the Boarding House the man behind the desk jumped up, "you're not going to bring that man in here a bleeding all over the....," that was as far as he got.

Miss. Judy popped him with a sucker punch in the left temple and laid him out cold. A woman cleared her throat, "that was one hell of a punch, and I've been wanting to do that ever since we got married. Please put Mr. Brown in his room number four, it's straight down the hall."

While the Doctor patched up Jodie, Judy filled him in on what all had taken place since she had arrived in town. "It seems three of the head tellers were more than willing to help put Mr. Biddingsworth in jail. His plot to rob several people was uncovered real quick. Most of the money had been recovered. But the bad side of things was, no Mr. Biddingsworth. He had disappeared the night after I and my twenty five trouble shooters arrived in town. It seems he was the ring leader of a gang of road bandits who called themselves the Red Scarf Gang. His second in command was none other than good old Mr. Wills. According to the newspaper, this same gang had a few days earlier gotten themselves all shot up by the now famous Jodie J. Brown and his three well decorated by the South for bravery, cousins, Mark E. Rollins, Jim D. Rollins and Harley H. Rollins, all three of Homes County. Mr. Golfer started this story off with how you had just survived the worst storm in history."

"The newspaper in Tallahassee went out and met the three Rollins brothers just before they reached Tallahassee and got their version of the big battle on the Tallahassee trail. Judy added as she pulled out a paper. "Let me read how they put it, I quote: Lance Corporal Harley H. Rollins the younger of the Rollins brothers told how the famous woodsman Jodie L. Brown joined the battle yelling like a Company of Rebels at Bull Run with his six gun a blazing and killing every bandit that got in his sights. End quote; Jodie you've got to slow down. I'm going to be gray headed before I'm Twenty One," said Judy as she finished telling them everything.

There was a light tap at the door, "Come in." called the Doctor as he finished with Jodie. It was James, "Mr. Jodie the marshal sent me to tell you that if you could walk, walk yourself over to his office. If you can't walk have somebody carry you, says he has a need to be talk to ya."

As Jodie walked through the door of the marshal's office he asked, "How's the bullet hole?"

"It hurts like hell. How's yours?"

"It couldn't be better. Set down boy, have a cup of coffee. Have you been filled in on the banker yet?"

"Pretty much, so marshal what do you think?" Ask Jodie as he eased down into a chair.

"I think there's still four more of those varmints out there and their held up somewhere near the rail road tracks awaiting for the train to take off back North, and I think they are going to board her just before she gets up a full head of steam. Also their thinking, they're going to make a clean get away."

"When do you reckon their going make their play?"

"Tonight, or should I say in the morning, the train leaves for Valdosta Georgia sometime around three am." Answered the Marshall as he polished his badge.

"What makes you think there's more than just the banker marshal?" Asked Jodie.

"There is no possible way he is in all this alone. T'aint possible he was that good. I know of at least three varmints missing besides the banker, because I have been quietly asking about town."

"I see, just how do you want to do this?"

"Well the way I see it," said the Marshall rubbing his chin absently, "they are going to come aboard the train through the back door. I'll be setting in the back seat like I'm a sleep. You're a going to be in the front seat doing the same. They will pass by me and take a seat somewhere between us."

Jodie smiled slyly and said, "you sly old fox, we are going to get them in a cross fire ain't we?"

Marshall Peabody

"You got that right Mr. Brown. I've already made arrangements for us to board the train around one thirty in the morning. So get you some sleep. We got us a long day tomorrow."

Jodie slid his chair back grunting in pain as he stood up; "I'll see you around one thirty, Boss Man."

A light mist was falling the next morning when the marshal tapped on Jodie's door. The only noise the marshal heard was a very faint squeak from a floor board and the door eased opened. Jodie was standing there ready. His six shooter was on his right side and his Bowie knife on his left and his repeater cradled in his left arm. "Damn boy you expecting a war or something?"

Jodie looked at the marshal, "just looking for the bastard that tried to harm my little sister and ordered the death of my folks."

The marshal smiled, "Oh! What the hell, if you want to kill him, or if you think you have to kill him, go ahead and do it. But Judge Tuner asked me if it was possible bring them in alive. He kind of wants to hang them." Cackled the Marshall, "he is getting cranky in his old age... But I never said it..."

"How about you Marshall, what do you want to do?"

"I'd sort of like to hang the varmint with my old cow rope then retire the rope. So if you shoot a few holes in him it'll be okay. His boots will still go flying through the air when I walk that old gray out from under him."

Jodie took in a deep breath and laughed trying to hold his side still; "you sure got a way with words marshal."

The two of them had just climbed aboard the train and took their places, the marshal at the back door and Jodie at the front, when the engine suddenly let off steam and belched out black smoke and started moving. And to all appearances she was headed north, all the way out of town, no one would guess that the plan was when it was all over, then the engineer would have to stop and back up all the way back into town to let the marshal and Jodie and maybe a few prisoners off.

Old Jack was right on time. The marshal looked at his watch, three o'clock on the dot. The Engineer bumped his whistle three times just to let the world know he was leaving town. Then the train jumped forward and started moving a little faster. The marshal was all balled up in a blanket Jodie was the same, they both had their six shooters at the ready. Someone running up behind the train yelling out, "Damn you Biddingsworth you said this was going to be easy."

"Shut up Robbins and give me your hand. Okay! Let's get inside before somebody spots us. Johnson you and Schoull grab a seat in the middle of the car. Robbins and I will take a seat across from you."

As they passed the marshal one of them blared out, "who the hell is that?"

Biddingsworth grabbed him by the shoulder, "shut up you fool we're on our way!"

"That was purity smart of you to buy these tickets Biddingsworth when the trouble first started."

"Yaw, but I don't think it was a good idea to kill the Brown family. If we'd left them till later that boy showing up wouldn't have hurt us." Gripped out Schoull, as he slouched down in his seat and pulled his hat low on his face.

"Oh hell, Schoull stop your crying. If things hadn't gone bad, and you sorry excuses had killed that snotty little Julie girl like I ordered, when I ordered, then we all four would be plenty rich off all the land we were stealing."

All at once the train screamed to a lurching stop.

Biddingsworth jumped up, "what the hell is going on?"

The marshal stood up, "you boys a planning a little trip?"

Biddingsworth went for his gun. The marshal was faster; his forty five came to life, as it belched out nine inches of blue flames. The banker was less one thumb. One of the others tried to run past Jodie only to get himself knocked in the head with the barrel of Jodie's 45 Long Colt, the man dropped like he was lead. By now Jodie had closed the gap between him and the third man; the man started reaching for his pocket pistol; "go ahead I wish you would!" Growled Jodie. The man lost his nerve and dropped to the floor with his hands on the back of his head. The marshal took out number four just as the train came to a complete stop. It was all over as fast as it started.

By now Jodie was in Biddingsworth's face, "I want to kill you so bad right now that I can't see anything but red... But I am not going to end your suffering that quickly, I want to watch you hang..." He spat out as he got a grip on himself, and backed away, before he gave into the killing lust and the revenge for his family that was screaming through him.

Biddingsworth, laughed and started to answer him when the Marshall smacked him in the mouth with the butt of his gun. "Shut up! You damn fool, I ain't ever seen someone walk that close to death and live through it."

The sun was just turning the sky orange when the marshal and Jodie started unloading their prisoners. Mr. Golfer was the first one there to meet them, "okay boys what's the scoop? I want to get it all in the morning news."

The marshal smiled at Mr. Golfer, "I'll leave it to my deputy, he's better at telling big whoppers than me.

Jodie looked at the marshal, "chicken. Well! Mr. Golfer the marshal as you know called me to his office yesterday. That's when he let me in on his plan on how he was going to catch these varmints. He laid out in detail about the train setup, where he wanted me and where he would be. It was as if he read their minds. They caught the train just as he said they would, everything went just as he said. They did give us a nugget, they confessed to killing the Brown family, Juley's and my folks. They also confessed to stealing a lot of land for personal gain, said they were planning on getting rich off the suckers of Ocala."

"What happened to the banker's hand?"

"He tried to out shoot the marshal, so the marshal shot his thumb off. I tell you Mr. Golfer it was like one those gun fighter books about the West. The marshal's gun came up out of its holster like magic and fired at the same time separating the banker's thumb from the rest of his hand. Yes sir. Mr. Golfer,

Marshal Peabody had old Biddingsworth figured out right from the start."

"Did you have to use your gun?"

"Only when I knocked that fellow in the head with it, and I feel real bad about doing that."

"Whys that?

"Because I think he's a going to be a little luppey from now on." Stated Jodie.

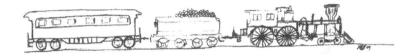

THE HANGING

Chapter Twelve

By the end of the week reporters were coming from around the Globe. Just about every country had reporters taking notes and asking questions. More telegraph lines had to be put in. Ocala, Florida was now on the map. Every day the prisoners were walked around certain streets under special guards that the Government had sent.

The Governor sent a special crew to build a gallows.

Judge Tunner was appointed Federal Judge. So he would be running the trial. Jodie was appointed a Federal Marshals position and Federal Marshal Henry J. Peabody got plum upset because he wasn't allowed to walk the old gray from under the sheriff or anyone else. He wasn't even allowed to pull the lever and drop any of those varmints through the trap doors. So he made sure he told everyone of them he was going to piss on their graves after they hung.

Marshal Peabody marched the first six up the gallows exactly six months after their capture, on November the third 1874. The rest of the gang members were hung three months later on February the third 1875, the day the church bells rang all day.

The day that Biddingsworth's trial started, he broke down and started confessing to all the people his gang had robbed and killed. The Judge ordered him to be taken out and be hanged by the neck until all the life left his body. And closed his Court by saying, may God have Mercy on your Soul. He was to die in two days.

Jodie was standing in front of the Court House thinking, "it's over now, and the dead could rest in peace." He looked down the street; a lone rider was slowly riding toward him. "James?"

"Howdy Jodie."

"What you doing in town James?"

"Paw sent me ahead of the family so I could find us a fitting camping place."

"Your whole family is coming to town?"

"Looks like, Paw said they wouldn't miss this shindig for anything."

Jodie thought he was talking about the hanging. Off in the distance you could hear a lot of black powder shooting going on.

"What you reckon all that shootings all about, Jodie?"

"Folks at the carnival are having a shooting contest."

"You recon I can go and have me a look?"

Jodie stepped out on the street, "tie your horse up here and let's find out." As they headed for the carnival Jodie got to looking at the long gun James was carrying on his shoulder, "when did you kill your last bear with that gun?"

"Yesterday I got me a big old Bear right in the middle of our camp."

"How did you bust your stock?"

"I fell out of a big Pine Tree a couple of years ago. Paw wrapped it with a piece of sheet copper and nailed it with shoe nails. It's a little shaky but it still gets the job done. All the family tells me I should be a getting me another one, but heck fire I wouldn't even know where to start looking for a gun like this."

They were just starting to get ready for the big shooting contest when the two of them got there. The first thing James seen was the first prize, a brand new Fifty Cal. black powder long gun.

"Hey Jodie what you reckon their going to do with that pretty gun over there?"

"They're going to give it to the best shot around these parts."

"Jodie, am I from around these parts?"

Laughing Jodie replied "You are that James."

"You think I can I have a shot?"

"Talk to that big man setting on that stool over there."

In a few moments James returned with a strange look on his face. 'Jodie what's two bits?"

"It is twenty five pennies, why?"

"The man said it would cost me two bits a shot."

Jodie reached in his pocket and pulled out a quarter, "here you go. This will pay for your first shot."

James handed the man his two bits.

"You get the last shot in the first go-around."

He quickly looked at Jodie.

"You shoot last."

James smiled, "I like that."

Everyone was looking at James's gun. One big mouth said "damn boy you really going to shoot that piece of junk?"

Jodie saw the fire spring up in James's eyes, "its okay James, I'll handle this". Jodie placed his hand on the man's shoulder; "this is the man that saved the famous Jodie Brown's life in the big shoot out at Silver Springs, you don't want to get him mad."

"Who the HELL are you anyway?" The big mouth growled.

"I'm Jodie L. Brown Why?"

"Sorry Mr. Brown it won't happen again."

It took a lot of time for all forty eight so called sharp shooters to get a turn. After everyone got a shot, the three Judges sorted the targets when they came to James target they looked at it and laid it aside. The rest they went over and over till they finally had James's and three more. They called out the four names, "okay you four line up right here. That will be two more bits each." Jodie handed James another quarter.

The Bear Slayers Gun

A man standing nearby said, "Boy that was one hell of a lucky shot. You will never make two of them in a row. And I've got money to back me up."

Jodie said, "Just what do you have in mind?"

"How about fifty dollars?

"That will do if that's all you got."

"I suppose you've got more." The man answered back.

About that time Judy walked up, "he's got just about a million dollars, how much did you want to lose?" She said as she slipped her hand in Jodie's.

"Naw! I think fifty dollars is fine..."

"Done!" Jodie said and shook his hand.

"Okay line up, it's time to see who is going to take this fine smoke pole home with them." One of the judges called out.

The first one fired, a big part of the bull's eye diapered. The second one fired another big part of the bull's eye diapered. The third man fired, the judge yelled out "almost perfect."

James stepped up to the line looked at Jodie, "the rifle is mine."

When the butt of his gun touched his shoulder he touched the trigger. The judge called out "perfect shot."

James turned and handed his old rifle to Jodie, "please hang it over the fire place in that Stake House of Juley's." He walked over and picked up the new rifle.

The big man got up, "there's more son, hold up. If you can shoot the new rifle as good as you shot your old one you get ten pounds of lead ball and ten pounds of round nose bullets plus five pounds of powder."

James looked at Jodie with a puzzled look, "what the heck did he say?"

"If you can shoot the new rifle as well as you shot the old one, he'll give you all those bullets and that can of powder." Jodie answered as he collected the fifty dollars from the bet.

James picked up the rifle took off his powder horn, put some powder down the barrel, laid a small piece of cloth over the muzzle, placed a led ball on top of the cloth and pressed hard on the led ball then took the ram rod and shoved it down till it rested on top of the powder, then placed a cap on the nipple.

"Well let's find out just how good the Bear Slayer really is."

"What did you just call him Mr. Brown?"

James smiled at the man, "I am the Bear Slayer." James turned and squeezed the trigger and the center of the target vanished. James was standing there smiling and shaking everyone's hand.

"James" Jodie called. "Here is fifty of this betting money is yours."

"I ain't ever had money like that." Gasp James.

"Well enjoy son you done earned it"

A pretty young girl with long pigtails eased up beside him and put her arms around his neck, "darn you Prissy you just scared two years of life out of me. What are you doing in town?"

"All us Seth's are in town for the big shindig. And I know I'm the best looking girl in the whole wide world because you told me I was."

"James, who's your friend?" Jodie asked holding back a smile.

"This here's Prissy Ann Seth."

"Hello Prissy."

"Hi, did James tell you we're going to get married some day?"

"No he didn't. Jodie answered hiding his laugh with a cough.

"Well we are I almost had him talked into kissing me on the lips the other day."

"What happened? Coughed out Jodie.

"A darn bear ran through the camp and he took out after it, so ended my almost first kiss." Sighed Prissy.

Judy smiled, "don't you worry Prissy there will be lots of other times."

"Oh you can bet your opossum hides on it. That husband is not a getting away from me. God made us for those Cone boys

121

and those Cone boys for the Seth girls. He's got no other chosen. And that's a fact." Stated Prissy.

James protested but not real hard, "Oh yaw!

"Yaw, so come on."

"Where are you taken me?" James protested as she dug him along with her.

"Home for something good to eat dad burn your rusted hide."

"Oh, what we having?" The two of them walked off holding hands. James had his new rifle and Prissy had the hand of her man.

Jodie smiled, "now that's what loves all about. Lots of yes I cans and no you can't's!"

After the hanging, Jodie was walking toward the Boarding House and was thinking "where's all the people all of a sudden? I wonder what's going on. The streets were pretty quiet for the time of day considering there had just been a hanging."

All at once he heard in a real soft voice, "Hey hayseed where you going? Want to have a little fun? Come with me I'll show you a wonderful time."

He looked all around; finally he spotted a small woman's hand sticking out of an alley waving for him to come. He checked his hand gun and headed for the alley. Once he reached the alley there was no one in sight. He slid the Colt out of the holster and slowly started checking each window and door as he made his way to the other end. When he walked out of the alley he muttered, "Well at least I found all the people."

Everyone was running around preparing for some kind of party. He spotted Juley, "hey sis what's going on?"

She smiled, "you'll know soon enough. Judy said for you to come in the livery stable as soon as you got here."

"What the devil does she want me in there for?"

"I don't know you'll have to ask her."

He walked off kicking rocks. He shook his head and mumbled, "For Havens sakes what's gotten into every one." The big doors of the stables were closed. By the time he reached them he was just about upset. He just snatched them open!

"Surprise!!!" A giant wedding cake was setting in the middle of the room. Mr. Willams took him by the arm and lead him over to Marshal Peabody who marched him to a large platform in the front of the room. "Oh by the way if you're wondering, I am your best man."

All at once a piano started playing the Wedding tune. The huge doors swung open once again. Mr. Williams was escorting Judy slowly through the doors; she was dressed in a lily white gown with a long train strung out behind her. She was beautiful, Juley and Peggy Sue was her maids of honor. A little girl was throwing rose peddles in front of Judy. Jodie was having trouble breathing, his heart was racing fit to burst and his legs threatened to collapse.

The preacher was standing there when Jodie turned around he was wearing a white shirt and a pair of bibbed overalls and a pair of brogans. The Bible he was holding under his arm must have had a thousand sermons preached out of it and he must have preached every one of them. Jodie thought, "How's he keeping that Bible held together?"

About that time two young boys came running in carrying a pulpit that looked as old as his Bible. He felt Judy slip her hand in his, when he looked in her eyes he knew everything would be all right.

Then a booming voice rang out, "Jodie do you take Judy to be your loving wife?"

"I do."

"Through sickness and in health till death do you part?"

"I do."

"Judy do you take Jodie to be your loving husband?"

"I do."

"Through sickness and in health till death do you part?"

"I do."

"What God has joined together let no man cast asunder. You may kiss your Bride. I now pronounce you man and wife." He smiled at the new couple and said, "Let the celebration began."

The Preacher shook Jodie's hand, "I knew your folks well. We prayed many a time that God would give you back to them. Your folks never thought for a moment you were dead. They were hard working folk that never knew what giving up was and they never stopped going till the job was done."

"I got here a little late Preacher." Jodie replied.

"Jodie with God everything is on time. So you arrived on time, right when God planned."

The marshal walked up, "Preacher Billings don't you know you can't save the right hand of the devil?"

"Marshal Peabody I can't save anybody. But you know Jesus can do all things, even save both the Devil's hands."

The marshal smiled and said "I'll see you in church Sunday, Rev."

The marshal handed Jodie a piece of paper, "what's this?"

"Heck I don't know Boy, you read better than me. I hardly read a taw."

"Yeah? Well I don't read a taw either." Jodie laughed.

"But that there paper looks mighty important, you best be getting that new wife of yours to read it to you."

Judy kissed him on the cheek, "here let me help you."

~ ~ ** ~ ~

ATTENTION: U.S. Marshal Jodie Lee Brown:

You have been assigned to Tallahassee, Florida.
Your new office is located at U.S. Offices Street.
Building #6, Room #77.

Reporting Date: June 15, 1875.

President <u>Ulysses S. Grant</u>.
The Year of Our Lord 1875...

P.S. Have a nice honey moon Officer. And tell my niece to enjoy my famous Marshal. Just make sure he's able to do his job when she returns him to duty.

You two enjoy yourselves. Lots of love.

~ ~ ** ~ ~

As Judy finished the letter, Jodie took her hand and drew her to him, "well let's go."

"Where are we going?"

"You're going with me."

"So I guess I'll be going with you to Jacksonville, Florida and catch a sailing ship to New York City. From there we'll follow a star to eternal love, till Gabriel blows his horn to come home." Judy stated as she snuggled closer to Jodie.

"Yep! That sounds about perfect to me." Jodie replied kissing her cheek.

"Well whatever you two love birds do, don't forget your reporting date. I don't want to have to track you down." Grunted the Marshall.

"Oh! Marshall..." Said Judy as she walked over to him. "You know you love us" and kissed his cheek as she danced away laughing.

"Hey now!" Roared the Marshall swiping at her, trying not to laugh. "Don't you be sassy now girly.. Get on out there so the town can say their goodbyes and wish you wells."

Together hand in hand Judy and Jodie went out into the sun set, into their future.

So begins the next chapter in their lives...

Jodie And Judy's Wedding

THE END

A SHORT STOREY BY JIMMYGRAYEAGLE

A Letter Home…